An
AMERICAN STORY

Emergent Literatures

An
AMERICAN STORY

Jacques GODBOUT

Translation by
Yves
SAINT-PIERRE

UNIVERSITY of MINNESOTA PRESS, Minneapolis

Copyright ©1988 by the University of Minnesota
Previously published as *Une histoire américaine*, copyright © Editions
du Seuil, 1986.

Published by the University of Minnesota Press
2037 University Avenue Southeast, Minneapolis, MN 55414.
Published simultaneously in Canada
by Fitzhenry & Whiteside Limited, Markham.
Printed in the United States of America.

Library of Congress Cataloging-in-Publication Data

Godbout, Jacques, 1933–
  [Histoire américaine. English]
  An American story/Jacques Godbout; translation by Yves Saint-
Pierre.
    p. cm. — (Emergent literatures)
  Translation of: Une histoire américaine.
  ISBN 0-8166-1709-0   ISBN 0-8166-1710-4 (pbk.)
  I. Title. II. Series.
PQ3919.2.G55H5713   1988
843 — dc19   88-4737
                                                                   CIP

The University of Minnesota
is an equal-opportunity
educator and employer.

An

AMERICAN
STORY

Chapter 1

The first day (he'd been arrested right at bath time)
Gregory witnessed the planting of an old, scrubby date
palm, in front of his window. All its life, in the deep heat
of Death Valley, the tree had brought forth juicy, sweet,
and mild fruit, with oblong dry pits that yielded easily to
the tongue. The Public Works Department of the State of
California, using a powerful crane hitched to a blue
truck, was transplanting it from the desert to serve as
decoration in the barren prison yard. The date palm was
so heavy that gardeners, with shovels, had to cover over
the sixteen wheel prints fanning out behind the platform,
where the eight pairs of wheels had sunk into the yellow
mud.

 While the work was going on, he tried to remember a poem, learned long ago in high school, in which
"palm" was rhymed with "calm." But his mind was lulled
to dullness by the palpable silence of the prison. Later, before darkness had entirely set in, the roof-top spotlights
bathed in a brash light the yard and the tree that would
never sleep again. Gregory himself slept lightly and
fitfully in the green neon of the night lights.

 The next day at noon a guard handed him some

documents in a gilded brown plastic binder held together by red and black rubber bands. He didn't open it immediately, as if delaying could impede the progress of administrative bureaucracy. He didn't want to know. He'd been thrown in jail without appeal, and he suspected the binder contained the opening chapter of a story that would slip completely beyond his control.

He was falsely accused (by the Republic, the State, and by district attorney Robert Roenicke) of two crimes: the violent rape of one Cheryll Wilson, nineteen, one hundred-thirty-two pounds, light complexion, thick, auburn hair. He'd allegedly lured the biotechnology student into the campus's Botanical Garden and attacked her on February 29 of the current year. There followed the victim's incoherent description of the way she'd been roughed up, choked, beaten, stripped, and threatened. Under a Japanese prune. Since the painful incident, she was subject to recurrent bouts of aphasia.

The accused was advised that the victim's parents had retained the services of a famous Los Angeles law firm specializing in particularly gory and sensational crimes. He immediately thought of the Charles Manson trial; he'd heard Manson interviewed on the radio in February, on the anniversary of Sharon Tate's death. Manson had answered the reporter's questions from prison, by telephone. Showbiz.

According to the second accusation, a few days later, on the morning of March 7, Gregory Francoeur had set fire to one of the buildings of the Nuclear Physics Research Center, situated east of the Lawrence Hall of Science, not far from the very same Botanical Garden. He'd gained entry into the court with wire cutters and suffocated the guard dog with an orange-colored polystyrene bag similar to those sometimes used by service crews to collect garbage alongside highways. Since the building also housed the data center, the damage was considerable. The nuclear physics research program was sponsored by the army. The file contained black and white photographs of the charred remains of a building of no particular style.

He considered the first accusation repugnant. The other, although he found it mildly amusing, was by far the more serious. Somebody was obviously out to destroy him, to smear his name completely. Rapist, arsonist. Would he have to stand two trials? The rape charge alone could bring ten years, not counting the claim for medical and psychological damages. And Roenicke had said arsonists were usually committed to institutions. Maybe a military mental institution.

In his wildest most pessimistic dreams, he'd never conceived of ending his days in a prison surrounded by transplanted date palms, or of being granted the dubious honor of becoming the first tenant in a brand new apple green stucco wing that still smelled of latex and carpet glue.

After he'd closed the binder, he spent a long time staring blankly at the grillwork on the window, the thick glass out of reach in its concrete frame. The air-conditioning made him shiver. He thought how colossal, how complete, how awesome the error was. He'd never raped anyone, not even in his most secret fantasies. Father.

"In school, I refused to join the soccer or lacrosse teams. I enjoy neither hitting nor being hit. I've never behaved violently, not even toward animals. The violence my words might have stirred was never more than polemical. Even my intimate relationships with women were always simpler and more wholesome than Roenicke's allegations suggest!"

On the third day he received a visit from the prosecutor: a pleasant fellow, youthful forties, on his way up, dreaming more of politics than of law, gray-blond hair, clean shaven, and wearing a dash of Eau Sauvage. They evaluated each other as they spoke, testing, eye to eye, barely scratching the armor. Teeth bared.

Gregory unexpectedly received special considerations: three weeks' grace (and solitude) in a sparkling cell, next to the institution's library. He could write up his own version of the facts. When he was first interrogated, they'd wanted to know exactly who he was, what he was doing in California, the involvement of the people close to him, his comings and goings. He'd record all of this in his journal. He was permitted to write in French; someone (perhaps a colleague from the university) would translate his notes for the jury and the investigators. The discussion about whether he should be allowed to prepare for his trial in his mother tongue delighted him. "I'll have carried the language struggle from the Atlantic to the Pacific!" he thought with relish.

Indeed, the fact that he was a foreigner and a guest of the state university had much to do with Roenicke's decision. Francoeur was also something of a television personality. The nobility of sword and cape having long since given way to that of diplomas and the media. But only when he made reference to his position as an ex-member of the National Assembly did the prosecutor commiserate, in hushed admiration, with his protestations of innocence. As a matter of routine, the San Francisco vice squad had contacted the police in Montreal. Francoeur had never been arrested or convicted, had no criminal record, and had only two demerit points for having exceeded the speed limit one night in a national park. A clean slate.

Although the metaphor didn't please him, he felt he had to fight back "like the devil in a tub of holy water." First, he had to have the rape charge dismissed. Because in these morality questions, right from the outset, the accused is never entirely innocent even in the eyes of his own mother. Who can claim to be without sin? Above all, he had no desire to play the victim in some ritual. As Catholics need periodic feasts to the virgin, so Protestants need to condemn, at regular intervals, either a fireman for an act of gross indecency in the fire hall, or the father of a large family for incest while under the influence of alcohol, or a mentally impaired pederast for infanticide in the midst of a heat wave, or a foreigner (Iranian, African, Mexican) for sexual assault. "I will not be the sacrificial rapist." He'd always been in close touch with his subconscious. Pop psycho.

"Maybe you've gone California crazy?" suggested the prosecutor as he handed him two ballpoint pens and a thick pad of cheap, yellow, legal-sized paper. Between you and me. Between us politicians, the hearty Roenicke must have been thinking.

"California crazy!" he wrote at the top of the first page of his journal. "I'm not crazy and I won't plead jungle madness. California frenzy, the machine-gunning of innocent and famished McDonald's patrons, razor blades in supermarket produce, strychnine-laced candy, blood lust, and the passion to become an omnipotent millionaire, does not, as far as I know, afflict one like some virus, the moment one steps off the plane!

"I was born in Montreal, Canada, forty-eight

years, eleven months, and two days ago. I can be accurate. My father, Georges-Henri Francoeur, was, for his entire working life, a sales rep for Larousse, the dictionary publishers whose famous trademark is the dandelion sowing in every breeze. My Irish mother named me for her first lover. She was tennis champion of eastern North America in 1935 before she became pregnant. I studied, played, learned my words and about life in the encyclopedias Father lugged to the courts, where Mother slugged to achieve the dreams of the athletic class.

"When I was still very young I became well known in the world of communications. At thirty I was reborn, thanks to television. I won a few *Coq d'Or* awards for my advertising and public relations campaigns. I loved Voltaire. I owed the inspiration for my characters to La Bruyere, and my slogans were borrowed from the locution of taverns. Those were the days when letters were respected and language was an art.

"But all this is probably of little interest to you."

He wondered whether he shouldn't adopt a more formal tone, perhaps a little grandiloquent, better suited to his defense. The language of lawyers. Wouldn't he have to plead his case, influence people? Could he muster the skill to persuade the prosecutor? It occurred to him that he'd never cheated before. People liked him straight, the way he drank his scotch. He would simply invite the reader to share his thought process and his actions, his uncertainties and his memories. The jury was only a group of anonymous amateurs, all of them for the moment wearing the face of Roenicke. Was his life at stake? Alas Vegas! Let the roulette wheel spin.

"I'm in California by chance and not as the result

of some Machiavellian plan. I did not come to Lotus Land to satisfy my repressed sexual urges or to threaten the security of the State. I don't properly understand where or how this story began. Perhaps the combination of a crisis of the heart and a crisis in politics. I came to California to cogitate in the sun. I've been thrown into darkness.

"Married, with one child, I'm now separated. From advertising I made the jump into active politics, but I've since resigned my seat and left the party. I felt I had the makings of a minister; the premier didn't concur. The boundary separating our collective adventure from my private life has always been as indistinct as a foggy day. In those days, the things we were experiencing as a people had a direct impact on my personal life. And I have to confess that, with regard to collective projects, our home province has been rather hard to bear these last few years. I'd taken on the people's cause like a huge advertising campaign. The consumer had ceased to respond.

"For months the entire land had been impassioned with the idea of independence; video cameras sprang up on street corners, in corridors, among a forest of microphones.

"It was the topic of every conversation. But you can't spend your life in a state of constant nationalist tumescence, living on promises and for futures never realized. My goal in politics had been the happiness of the people. We were bullied, and in a schizophrenic vote, the population defeated itself. Fiasco. Debacle. Detumescence. The foreign press packed up their gear and turned out the spotlights; the show was over.

"Once again we'd been satisfied with singing the roughed out melody of a utopia. It became obvious that we would never achieve the final draft of independence. It was a helium dream, devoid of deep desire. Afterward, it all came apart, strand by strand, like a rotten rope. So did my marriage. But I wasn't the only one: after the referendum many couples broke up because they had nothing more in common. Misery and monotony were everywhere.

A few months later, I left the party. The membership had become as irascible and belligerent as so many Paris cabbies. The younger ones spoke avidly of joining the jet set. When your spirits are sagging, a face-lift is still a lift of sorts. The nationalist question no longer interested anyone but the old party faithfuls, who would gather, after dark, and dance to the reels of Saint-Dilon and Saint-Jean-Baptiste, and to the tune of the old veterans' gigue."

Then autumn came, with November holding the promise of winter. Bitter cold, glacial winds, sleet, and wall-to-wall gray clouds. For two years Gregory had not held a steady job. Now and then he'd give a lecture or do a radio show for the paycheck. Occasionally he'd guest host a television public affairs program. He was, however, better known than rich. And when he drank the fruits of his labor, in the company of friends, behind the windows of cafés on Saint-Denis, he found himself stating, between sips of Beaujolais nouveau riche, that Quebec's future lay with the United States. New fervor. Keep the money rolling. Montrealers are severe manic-depressives.

"That's when I received an unexpected offer: the American Association of Social Communicators invited me to spend six months, the winter-spring semester, in San Francisco. I'd been general secretary of the association eight years before, and that volunteer service had paid off at last. Sufficient salary, a research project, a few classes to supplement the month's earnings. It seemed a great chance to distance myself from raw politics, to plunge completely into theory, to undergo a needed transfusion, perhaps even to appropriate a new patrimony before I turned fifty. After all, I might decide to stay in California."

In fact, Gregory had thought about it seriously as a chance to emigrate. But the formalities proved to be long and complicated, and the immigration officer so unpleasant, he ended up soliciting only a temporary work visa. Like most Canadians, all he knew of California were the mythical images: beachboys and limousines, Napa wines and thousand-year-old sequoias. He couldn't even have said whether Berkeley, where he was to do his research, was near Hollywood. Some of his friends were frankly worried to see him go. Would they even recognize him when he came back? But, as the storms of December grew stronger, most envied him. The gossip columnist of a major daily predicted a prodigious turn in his career that would lead him to the big Hollywood studios.

Thinking about the weeks leading up to his departure, Gregory suppressed an angry gesture. The gossip had seen clearly into her crystal ball: this prison had some of the characteristics of a film set, all right, with its black spots mounted on movable scaffolding and its guards in quaint costumes. Now where could Fred Astaire have gotten to?

"I have friends who love to organize other people's lives. They showered me with useless recommendations, dangerous advice, and the addresses of new-age gurus. When I broke the news to my wife, she just laughed. My son didn't say a word: going to California befitted his age more than mine, that's what he wasn't saying. Suzanne laughed out of relief; she wouldn't have to put up with me anymore. My parents found the idea distasteful; they'd just bought a small retirement house in Provence. I'd chosen the wrong "côte d'azur." Dad had christened the place Villa la Rousse. The neighbors thought it was for my mother's flaming red hair. But he thought only of dictionaries. He always was a company man. I, a contradictious one. When Dad wanted to set me up in business, I became a missionary."

He recalled, nearly thirty years earlier, shaking with fear when he came before some forty Ethiopian students at University College in Addis Ababa, wearing a white tunic to protect his suit from chalk dust. He sported a thin mustache, as invisible as it was blond. A philosophy professor just turned twenty, he wore heavy-soled, maroon, English shoes too big for his feet. His students (primarily Muslims) were ten years older than he was. He had just lost his faith. He was more sure of himself than he had reason to be. He put all authors on the same shelf, and dusted off each of them, smiling the same skeptical smile.

How had he come to be behind this lustrous lectern? A philosopher? At his age? At the time he'd have done anything, tackled giants, played all the parts offered to him, learned all the codes, agreed to talk about nothing, sung to an empty house, simply to get away from the icy land of tuques and holy water.

He was born into an open-minded family bound up by a suffocating culture. And this unexpected contract with the Abyssinian Ministry of Education suddenly presented all kinds of possibilities: an advantageous marriage, a good salary, a trip across Europe in grand style, and a plunge deep into the heart of Africa at the expense of His Majesty, the most serene Haile Selassie. He wasn't really a teacher, only marginally a writer, a young poet in the mold of Rimbaud who'd only by chance heard of Harar. With equal measures of innocence and remorse, stepping squarely along the well-worn path of the Great Western Guilt, he was coming to "help the negroes" adapt to the modern world.

The first day of class, forty students wondered by what right this young white boy was standing at the lectern. He walked nervously to the window, wrote A — for Aristotle — on the blackboard, turned around, and withered. What was Aristotle doing in Addis Ababa? Was logic universal?

That night Suzanne had let the peas and carrots burn to the bottom of the aluminum pot while she listened to Gregory recite the catalog of his catastrophes.

Chapter 2

Of course, he hadn't come to help the Pacific Coast natives adapt to the technological revolution. California missions, with their Hispanic churches and manicured Indian cemeteries, have long been part of the tourist circuit, right up there with Disneyland. Fodder for the family album.

But Gregory could imagine himself bearing testimony, in his fashion, to French culture in America, perhaps through a politics and communications course. This time the students would be thirty years younger than he. Francoeur absolutely refused to consider that he might have accepted the AASC's offer for his *own* pleasure. He could never undertake anything that didn't have *societal* significance. He'd always sought to occupy that sacred ground where the public and private meet. He would give of himself and take at the same time, protecting his privacy with all his might, while he moved barefaced through the crowd. Bleeding heart.

Could this be happiness, the ultimate in Judeo-Christian pleasure? The unforeseen meeting of solitary joy and public reward? He had only one desire, to decipher the drumbeat messages of the local society, without intruding; to find his niche, and there, like a miraculous statue, to glow discreetly. This time he wouldn't wear a white lab coat, or bankers' shoes. He would present himself as a romantic citizen, a picture of studied neglect, vital organs full of phosphorous.

"I wouldn't want to resort to the mythology of witchcraft for an explanation, but is it possible for a magical bond to spring up spontaneously between a person and a place? Can a culture engender irreversible chemical processes? Can a person become a catalyzing agent in spite of himself? Within my first few hours in this country of excess, I perceived improbable relationships between the past and the future, beyond the oceans. A music with no vestige of logic, a preternatural harmony. Strange California. While Ethiopia cried famine, I could hear the fast-food stands, on San Francisco Bay, take up the collection. Very astutely, they were embracing a noble cause to boost sales."

Gregory Francoeur had always been more sensitive to ads and commercials than the average consumer envisioned by market research. This sensitivity had allowed him to perceive with unfailing accuracy the hidden slots in which to promote a given product. The winds of marketing blew stronger on the West Coast than in his land of snow. He was spinning like a weather vane.

"Dairy Queen, Burger King, and the rest invite you to eat hearty and fast; X percent of the proceeds goes to Africa! Customers bursting with fries and their own generosity go home and feed the cat or dog. But, unbeknownst to them, they're giving their pets banquets of wild flesh, canned pieces of gazelle or strips of zebra. Cat food. Dog food. Clear conscience? Elephant flavored.

Open a can of dog food at random, Pepper, Canigou, or Pal, and hold it up to your ear. You'll hear the echo of Tarzan's yell. The baboons' last sigh. The silence of the plain. In the papers, Ethiopia and famine make the front page. In supermarkets, Africa is on the shelves."

He was so moved when he remembered the posters in the restaurants showing the emaciated faces of Ethiopian children that he pursued his diatribe for a few more pages. Then he realized that his journal would be of little use to him if he carried on like this. The jury's duty was not to pass judgment on those responsible for the deaths of children in the desert but to decide on the allegations of rape and arson pending against him. The suffering of Cheryll Wilson was no small thing. A plague does not kill the masses, he thought, but individuals. He changed his tone.

"When I landed in San Francisco at the end of January aboard Air Canada's flight 759, on a Thursday morning, I was suffused by a pleasant exhaustion. In a final gesture of self-sacrifice, Suzanne had driven me to Dorval airport. Anyway, I was leaving winter and all that behind and emerging into radiant weather, all blue sky and soft sunshine. The first three nights I slept in a bed the size of a football field, at the Hotel Durant, on the street of the same name in Berkeley, where I'd been dropped by the airport connection's minibus. There were six of us aboard the minibus, disparate passengers thrown together only by the happenstance of travel. A very old Russian Jew was coming to join his children on the coast. The four others, two yuppie couples, were coming to romp on the beaches with the seals.

"From my seat beside the driver I could see the unspoiled (technicolor) vista of the waters of the bay, its wild ducks, the hills of San Francisco, Treasure Island, driftwood sculptures. I took in the view like a photo-electric cell feeding on light. It gave me an energy I'd never known before. At street corners I stared at the passersby, feasting on them with my eyes. I swallowed them like vitamin pills. I was finally comfortable being me. Free. Such a feeling could only be superficial, but you can't spend your entire life swimming only in the depths!"

As soon as he'd opened his bags at the Durant Hotel, Francoeur decided to blend right into the scene. He entered Henry's, the hotel's fake English pub, like a regular, and freely indulged in a crowd bath. He ordered the special of the day (sole with capers, broccoli, endives) and a bottle of Chardonnay. In Montreal he was unable to sit in a single bar without being subjected to someone's original opinions on the political situation. Here, he was anonymous. He sat for a couple of hours enjoying the chaos and the cries of students boisterously reunited after the Christmas break. But it was only an interlude. When he got the bill he multiplied by three meals, added the price of the room, calculated the exchange rate, and realized he wouldn't be able to enjoy hotel life very long. He'd have to start looking for a furnished apartment right away. For the first time in twenty-five years, Gregory Francoeur, newly become solitary bachelor, would have to deal with himself face to face.

A few weeks before he left, Suzanne had proposed separation as an alternative to divorce. They'd chosen Christmas to celebrate their sad but necessary decision. They both knew their love would not make it through another winter. His wife hated the idea of living in the States, even for a few months. But, of course, that wasn't why she was leaving him. She didn't want to have to deal with his mood swings anymore. Stop. Break. Enough. "Each of us alone at opposite ends of the continent and things should work out just fine."

"She had known my fears as a student, my anxieties as a teacher, my pretensions as an artist, my concerns as a creator, my promotional speeches, my theories on communication, my political ambitions. I'd been a fragile plant needing to be loved, watered, given light, repotted, exhibited, compared, and encouraged when autumn came."

Quite suddenly, Suzanne had had enough of playing horticulturalist. Maybe he'd been severely depressed for the last several months without admitting it even to himself. He was leaning more and more heavily on his wife: carry me! He was constantly pressing her, as the princess her mirror, to tell him he was the most handsome, the greatest, the strongest. She gave him his fair measure. She supported him when he tottered on the stilts of his vanity. But she could no longer lie to him; since he'd left politics Gregory had done nothing of any substance. His depression was contagious. He exhaled clouds of toxic dust. His saliva was turning to acid.

Suzanne's career, on the other hand, had been taking off, particularly over the last five years. A respected psychopedagogue, she was coordinator of many projects, swamped with research grants, and in constant demand at seminars and conferences on the exceptional child. She would often joke that Gregory alone had provided her with all the experience she needed. The invitation to California had arrived in the nick of time. The child Gregory had had enough of playing the eccentric traits of genius. Christmas Eve Suzanne and he had drunk champagne, as befit the occasion, had listened to old music, all bells and white snow, and had exchanged last gifts: a burgundy leather travel kit for Gregory, and for Suzanne, a framed photograph of him, to remind her. He'd gone to a professional portrait photographer who'd slipped a stool under his bum and a fake fence under his elbows and then pulled his face forward and half around. It looked like an ad for a vermifuge.

After their *réveillon*, Gregory had wanted to make love on the carpet beside the fetish *crèche*, at the foot of the lighted tree. Suzanne had called him an ass. The night had ended peaceably under the Christmas tree stars. In the end he'd gone alone into the freezing dawn, at once disappointed and elated. He was going to "make a man" of himself and sleep at his mother's until he left.

Trying to find an apartment, or even a room, in a West Coast university town like Berkeley, is quite an undertaking. He went to rental agents and placed a small ad at random among the hundreds of varicolored notes pinned like patchwork to the neighborhood telephone poles.

"Every morning there were dozens of immigrants: Tai, Poles, Japanese, Germans, Pakistanis, Brits, and others, all lined up to get the agent's latest list, all looking frantically for the ideal place. The prices were commensurate with the scarcity of apartments. For two days I walked all over the city, going from phone booth to futile visit, to: 'Sorry it's already rented,' to a refusal: 'You don't have references,' to a beautiful but unfurnished house, to a damp hole."

At the end of the second day, Gregory strayed into

a downtown lounge, the Santa Fe Bar and Grill, where cool Chablis was served in wine glasses in a railroad setting. The first Californian with whom he shared a toast (*Have a nice day.*), a drunk who was quaffing gallons of Gallo (*Have a nice drink.*), introduced him to a friend who had a solution to every problem. This man drove him out to Piedmont Street in his Porsche. Sitting at road level, wedged between hot mufflers, Gregory was given a ride in the most powerful car he'd ever been in. Even so, they reached their destination without exceeding the speed limit. The small house, all dark shingles, sat beneath damp foliage. It was separated from its neighbors by huge spiny bushes. In the yard stood a group of pines as lofty as ideals that protected it from the noonday sun. The whole thing suggested either the lair of some toothless witch or a crow's cabin straight out of an illustrated Grimm's.

"Well it was a roof, anyway! And available. At a reasonable price. With a little brick fireplace, dry wood stacked in the yard, a kitchen to clean, and a gas water heater. The owner, in Asia for an extended trip, had abandoned his huge Buick, under a gray dust cover, beneath a street light in front of the portico. Sparrows were nesting in it.

"I sublet it from a hustler, half superintendent, half student before the Eternal, who, in his spare time, was writing a master's thesis on 'The Concept of Freedom in the Works of Jacques and Raissa Maritain.' He also took out the garbage twice a week and tended the lawn and shrubs. He lived in a caretaker's lodge across the road.

"I signed a lease right on the spot as well as a few American Express checks, which he pocketed along with my business card. Out of politeness, I explained that I was undertaking research into the concept of happiness and that we should talk about it one day. He offered to show me one of those posh suburban subdivisions California developers build for adults only. Neighborhoods that bar couples with children must embody new concepts of happiness, he suggested, and I could begin my work with a comparative essay on the sensuous pleasures of the whirlpool as opposed to the joys of the (family) swimming pool. Moonfaced Maritain made a good case. Then, to put me at ease, no doubt, he added that Berkeley was still an open community and that I would feel right at home. "*Have a nice evening!*" He handed me the keys.

"I walked to the Hotel Durant and arrived a little after seven. The night clerk gave me an envelope along with my room key. It was a letter from my son. Or rather, a communication. Janvier (he was born in the heart of a blizzard) never writes, properly speaking, but now and again he slips into an envelope a press clipping that seems pertinent. It's a habit he picked up at his free school where, year round, the children devoted their time to "research" rather than to grammar. Suzanne and I were ardent defenders of alternative schools. They taught Janvier the masterful manipulation of scissors and a complete disdain for orthography. When he was a child, he took great joy in cutting up his grandfather's encyclopedias for school projects. Georges-Henri was not amused. Janvier could not understand why he wasn't allowed free access to primary sources. This time, the clipping from France-Presse originated from the Vatican. I read it while I was waiting for the elevator.

"(*AFP*) 'The devil really exists,' " according to German Cardinal Joseph Ratzinger, prefect of the Congregation for Doctrine, who made the statement on Monday. This honored prelate, responsible for the purity of the faith, stated that the devil is mysterious but real, a personal and not a symbolic presence. In an interview granted to the Catholic weekly *Jesus*, he went on further to qualify the devil as a palpable, powerful reality, capable of awful atrocities. 'As satanic cults multiply in the secular world, there are already signs of a return of the dark forces,' he added.

"Thus did Janvier express filial love. He wanted to warn me, thinking: these cults are particularly prevalent in California; you are no more protected against the forces there than are the superficial theologians denounced by Ratzinger who call into doubt the real presence of the devil; I'm sending you this news clipping, I didn't make it up; we never talk, you and I, and now you're alone in a dangerous world; I'm thinking about you, dear dad."

Gregory Francoeur knew that, above all, his son was totally devoid of humor. When he cut out a clipping, it was to be taken literally. So, a few minutes later, with the article still in hand, when he saw a young man as tall as a basketball player bashing his head against the wall of the elevator and whimpering like a man possessed, he thought Satan had indeed slipped in through the door. From drugs and deliria deliver us O Lord. He got off gratefully on the third floor. Drops of sweat trickled between his shoulder blades and he felt his collar was strangling him. *California crazy?*

He'd always been rather impressionable. The message from his son, probably mailed the day he left, was enough to make him pack his bags that very night. He took the two buffalo skin suitcases he'd bought from an Italian in Asmara, Erythria, which had proven indestructible through his entire marriage, and took the stairs down to the lobby to avoid the elevator. In a sweat, he asked for his bill. They charged him for the night; rather than protesting, he paid the whole thing.

In front of the hotel, a young, one-woman band was performing. On top of her Viking helmet, a red bulb flickered to the music while she played a transistorized synthesizer linked to two speakers and, with strings tied to her feet, a bass drum and a cymbal. She sang into a lapel mike with a voice from beyond, and the sound she produced was divine. Francoeur was overcome. A cardboard sign by the collection plate at her feet read "Live Aid for Africa." This luminous angel restored peace to his soul. A kind of joy. He would have liked to talk to the young lady, but she didn't even pause to catch her breath between songs. He threw in his offering, hailed a cab, and under a milky sky lit by a moon as glazed as an aspirin, returned to what would be his first bachelor lair.

Having been empty for several months, the place was cold and damp — tomblike. He felt exhausted all of a sudden, empty, incapable of getting wood or even of going down to the basement to turn on the gas. He hadn't put in a day of walking like that since he was a student in Paris. He locked the door, put his bags down in the foyer, and dragged himself up to the first floor. Wondering which, God or Satan, had died first in his life, he went into the largest of the three bedrooms and, without further ceremony, fell onto the bare, yellowed, and typically bloodstained mattress. He dropped off in the fetal position, wrapped in his beige trenchcoat as though in a sleeping bag.

"I didn't sleep that night, I just had nightmares: in order to complete my research on happiness, I had to interview ten dogs on leashes held by fat, gray-haired Africans. The walls were plastered with posters of Janvier as a rock star. I was having trouble with my work. I was in the back seat of a convertible, and Maritain was driving. At my side, Suzanne was typing my hypotheses on the go. At a corner we collided with the one-woman band, who'd moved onto the street. She was sent tumbling with her instruments. I jumped out and tried to help her up, but she slipped through my fingers like sand. A basketball player came by. He was passing out multicolored pills from the two halves of a severed ball. I took a handful, swallowed them, found myself in bed with the one-girl band while Suzanne played her instruments. I don't remember anything after that."

Chapter 3

When he woke up early the next morning, he wasn't sure where he was, in what city or room. Suddenly it dawned on him that what he'd thought to be gauze curtains in front of the windows facing the bed were, in fact, two *chammas* stretched on wooden poles. Sunday *chammas* with magnificently ornate gold and orange borders. He closed his eyes a moment and pictured the faraway figures of high plains Ethiopians wearing this white, togalike outerwear, one panel draped off a shoulder or drawn over the head as a hood. The men often held the hem in their mouths to protect themselves from the cold and from indiscreet looks. When Gregory opened his eyes again, he went over and felt the *chammas*. He rubbed the fabric between thumb and forefinger. Should the strange, unexpected presence of these light cotton garments worry him? Touching them was like recalling a scent from childhood, powerful and pleasant. Was it an omen? What could it mean? Of course the landlord could simply have traveled in Ethiopia, brought the garments back from Addis Ababa or Gondar, and then decided that they'd look good over the windows of his bedroom.

But that didn't make much sense. Few people visit

Ethiopia for pleasure. The overthrow of the negus had made touring rather difficult for the last few years. For months, under the tyranny of the Marxist colonels, every morning at dawn garbagemen filled wicker baskets to overflowing with severed human limbs. Forearms, heels, fingers, children's heads, sexual organs, shoulders, all cut as cleanly as sugar cane. Political autopsy.

Addis Ababa didn't appear on vacation brochures; Club Med hadn't made it one of its destinations. What exactly had this Californian been doing in the heart of Semite Africa?

"No doubt preparing, some twenty-five years later, a setting similar to that of my wedding, so that I could begin my bachelorhood under the auspices of the Lion of Judea."

Gregory felt dizzy. And he was overcome by memories he thought he'd relegated to the closet of forgotten emotions.

"Suzanne and I had worked so hard to try to transform that miserable earthen cabin into a space that felt like us. At the Mercato I'd bought red, blue, and yellow water soluble paint powders (one satchel to a pail of water), and I'd covered the rotting wallpaper. In the four corners we'd hung clay plates I'd decorated with faces inspired by Rouault. The effect was more symbolic than successful; the walls were streaked, the woodwork mottled, and in the humid half-light, the plates looked like scooped out hollows. But together we'd fashioned our first intimate decor. There would be many others."

It was a compulsion with him. To put his house and his things in order was to put his thoughts in order.

"At the Hotel Durant I could usually find some chambermaid or doorman to joke with. I realized however, that from this morning on I'd be talking to myself, like some abandoned old woman.

"Through the *chammas* I could see the turtledoves already chasing each other in the cruel morning sunlight. I wandered like a spider from room to room through the dead smell of the house. As I moved furniture much too heavy for me, I played different parts, changing my voice and answering myself from bathroom to livingroom. I was the Char, the Plumber, the Architect, the Decorator, the Disappointed Tenant, the Lost Child. The six of us did a good job. I was reminded of an article Janvier had cut out of a magazine for me in which a psychiatrist described the sixteen personalities of a schizophrenic patient. What fun it might have been for all of us to work together!

"A sleepy, gray, female cat and a tom with a coat as slick as a mink's were patiently waiting for me on the back porch. Maritain had explained that the discount I was getting on my rent carried the express condition that I feed the household felines for the absent landlord. The fridge was overflowing with tins of salmon and tuna. The kitchen cupboards were filled with bags of dry food. No *Sahel* here! I introduced myself. I'd been told her name was Kitty, his Lucifer. According to Maritain, Kitty was Lucifer's mother. It was hard to believe. He was a fright with his short, spikey tail. They observed me from a distance while I dished out their food. I added a bowl of fresh water and left them outside. Lucifer hissed at me. Watching them wolf their food made me hungry."

The residential neighborhood in which Gregory Francoeur's rented house stood stretched from the grounds of the Clairmont Hotel, a wonderful, huge, vaguely Victorian building, dressed entirely in white like an old-time tennis player, down to San Francisco Bay and the Berkeley pier. There being no provisions for a biped, he left cat haven and followed the natural incline of the sidewalk. He soon found himself on Telegraph Avenue, the famous commercial street that leads to the university and seems forever frozen in the hippy era of the sixties. Peace 'n love.

He yielded to the scent of warm dough emanating from Blondie's and ordered a slice of vegetarian pizza. It was served on wax paper. With his meal in one hand and a newspaper in the other, Gregory sat on a low wall in the sun and read the local news in the *Bay Guardian*. The lead story was as horrible as a fairy tale. "Butcher, butcher, who's in your larder?" He thought of Georges-Henri, then caught himself: he was not going to become like his son, Janvier. The week before he'd arrived, two young girls had been attacked with a knife. One was dead, the other would be in a wheelchair for the rest of her life.

Both were bright, private school students from good, well respected families. They'd taken advantage of an afternoon off to go wandering on the grounds of the mansion once owned by the heiress to the Pullman fortune. It was one of those crazy California extravagances, a baroque old home John Kennedy had once thought of making his "Pacific Whitehouse." It was said that the mansion, willed to the city ten years earlier and since then abandoned, was haunted by the ghost of guests who, seduced by the memories of grand soirees, refused to leave.

It was also said that there were treasures hidden somewhere in its fifty-three rooms and that, at night, the oaks on the vast grounds danced to the melodies of old time waltzes.

The two girls had first skirted the grounds and looked into the outbuildings. Then the watchman, dressed in the blue uniform of a city employee, invited them in to look for the ghosts of the Pullman mansion. Imagine how thrilled they must have been. The place was usually closed to the public. Could they hear, in the long hallways, echoes of the trains that made the original owners' fortune? The rhythm of the wheels on steel rails, the wind on the plains, and the lowing of buffalo? Were they saddened by the smell of decay emanating from the Victorian wall coverings?

A few minutes after they'd set foot in the hall, the watchman had attacked them with a knife, knocked them down, tied them up, and thrown them into the trunk of his fire-engine red Dodge Dart. Then, as he always did on Thursday, he'd gone to his sister's to play Monopoly. Marvin Gardens. *Do not pass go.* He'd lost the game, and, after a last beer, he'd gone home around midnight. He'd taken a canyon road and left the girls at the bottom of a ravine.

By dawn the next morning, according to the *Bay Guardian*, one of them had dragged herself to the roadside and been picked up by a motorist. Her hair was matted with mud and blood, and her shoulders were torn. She alerted the authorities to the whereabouts of her friend, and they were both taken to the hospital. The brave one who'd dragged herself hand over hand to the road died that night of blood loss. The smaller one, her spine injured, had lost the use of her legs forever.

"The watchman at the Pullman mansion, a black man in his thirties with broad shoulders and a bouffant hairdo, was arrested and jailed the next day. He's in the same prison I am, in an older wing facing mine. Sometimes I think I see his fist closed around one of the iron bars. As though he were waiting for death or for the walls to crumble.

"Today, at noon, I went to the prison library and found a number of pertinent facts. I read in a criminology quarterly that since the death penalty has been reinstated, of the fifty prisoners who have been electrocuted, gassed, or hanged, depending on the state, thirty-five were black. For every one hundred thousand Americans, statistics show that five hundred seventy-four blacks are in prison and only sixty-five whites. They'll have to add to their computerized figures one French Canadian, under the column headed: Dreams— *made in the U.S.A.*"

Keeping the journal and preparing his own defense was no mean task. Normally Gregory could have called for help and ten credible witnesses would have come running, prepared to swear before God there'd been a miscarriage of justice. But when Roenicke had asked for the names of close friends, he hadn't been able to supply a single one. Maritain? He knew him only by his nickname. Everyone in California lived in his own bubble, or in his car, eyes fixed on the traffic lights of his personal ambitions.

"Here, exchanges are brief, communications are civil, but no one gets involved on a personal level. It's no coincidence that new therapies are constantly being invented in California. Every massage is a way of avoiding contact. It's easy to feel like the global village idiot.

"For instance when I decided, that day at noon, to get in touch with Administration Services, I was astounded by the profound indifference with which I was received. I'd just arrived from the other end of the continent, I spoke a foreign language, I was an official representative of the association, responsible for an important research project on happiness approved by the communications department and financed by the humanities. It was an international project and here I was being treated like some no-account! I was not introduced to my new colleagues (some of whom are famous), ostensibly because I could be of no use to anyone."

The office was run by a very young woman, seemingly bent on denying her sexuality because she wore only baggy garments made of sweatshirt material. As she moved from the phone to the photocopy machine, she always seemed to be hesitating between running four hundred meters or going to the showers. Her greasy, flat hair held a pen and three pencils. She gave Gregory several forms to fill out: attestations of his various degrees, two sheets for internal revenue, an application for Social Security, a medical insurance form, and finally the one about next of kin to be notified in case of death.

When he was filling out this last form, Francoeur made his first mistake. He didn't give his parents' names because they'd moved to France. Nor did he give his wife's name since they'd just separated. "If Suzanne's had enough of me alive," he figured, "why should I burden her with my corpse? My son? He has other problems. He's an artist. The best I could do for him would be to commission a tombstone. But he carves in bone. Offer to leave him mine? Too morbid. When I left Montreal I'd burned my bridges, how could I possibly send a coffin back?"

Prosecutor Roenicke didn't see things in the same light. Gregory Francoeur had named as his executor and sole beneficiary one Rafael Ross, of the Ladd Society of New York. Their offices were on the fortieth floor of the World Trade Center. When he checked it out, Roenicke found that Rafael Ross was known to the police and was wanted for fraud in California. Francoeur's apparent association with Ross led the prosecutor to conclude that he belonged to an international gang. And if Gregory continued to deny knowing Ross, the fact that he willed his ashes to the Ladd Society would still indicate an erratic, even lunatic personality capable of any manner of deviant behavior.

"Roenicke is getting carried away. I didn't want my ashes sprinkled over the Golden Gate like some John Doe, and I was taken in by the beautiful four-color brochure and the personal letter addressed to the occupant I'd found in the house. I was seduced by the notion (and the idea did have merit) of donating my remains and the cash from my life insurance and from the sale of my few possessions to an outer space undertaker. It wasn't the first time I'd made purchases through direct mail. The oil companies that have sold me brass cookware, luminous globes, portable typewriters, and a thousand useless things could attest to that. Call Esso and Shell to the stand! I didn't want to be a problem to anyone. The cost of the enspacement — given that seven hundred urns are required to make a profitable launch to a twenty-eight-thousand-kilometer orbit — was only ten thousand dollars a pound! I'm not sure what my ashes will weigh, but that didn't seem an exorbitant price to pay for the comfort of floating near God in the fecund ether from which our world was born."

The administrator in sweats and Gregory Francoeur quickly came to an understanding regarding the practical details of his stay at the university. The department would provide the services of a part-time secretary, a pigeonhole for his mail, and access to the computer and telex machine. They also settled details regarding a telephone, his timetable, conference rooms, classrooms, audio-visual equipment, photocopying, and other such necessities. Office space was limited and that posed a bit of a problem, but he was offered the key to a room in a contiguous building; a room at tree-top level on the fourth floor, if that was satisfactory. In a way, that office is where his problems began.

"The fourth floor could be reached by a slow elevator or by a vast stairway. The stairway smelled of wax, the corridors of disinfectant, but when I opened the door of the office my throat was seized by the smell of peppermint and mildew. The dust of erudition floated in the air. Effluvia of the great masterpieces irritated my uvula and I was submerged in the subtle scent of ancient books.

"First I looked over the small bookcase leaning against the wall. It overflowed with varicolored, well worn volumes (*Introduction to French Masterpieces, The Life of Bernard Shaw, la Peste*). The office had been permanently assigned to a professor who, I was assured, used it only one morning a week. My invisible colleague apparently read French. Had this been a thoughtful consideration? His domain was to the left of the door. To the right of the window, a bare, gray table had been placed for my use. A piece of yellowed cardboard stuck to the frosted window by a strip of dried up tape gave the name of my absent colleague: Allan Hunger."

The old professor's desk (judging from the accumulation of dust and the incunabula, Francoeur guessed he must be about a hundred years old) was piled high with promotional brochures, students' papers, newspaper clippings, sports magazines, interdepartmental memos, posters announcing peace demonstrations, paper clips of all sizes, and unsealed letters. On the shelves and filing cabinets around it, precarious piles of files formed a miniature city in ruin. Allan Hunger seemed to cultivate absolute disorder. Obsessively.

"Messiness annoys me. Allan Hunger was already exasperating me. Having made a living at tennis, my mother had a predilection for clean surfaces, delineated spaces, white and clear. She nursed me in the stands at tournaments, first one nipple then the other, to the rhythm of the bouncing balls. Whack! Slurp! (Dangerous nursing. When a player missed a shot I sometimes missed the nipple, choked, and turned white as the ball.) I've kept from my childhood a love of precision, and I sometimes still hear the murmurs of the crowd punctuated by applause. Today when I hear applause I get an erection. I can't help it, it's a conditioned reflex. Success excites me. But disorganization drives me crazy.

"Perhaps that's why, those first few minutes in Allan Hunger's office, I behaved absolutely outrageously. I opened and went through all his drawers, I looked over all the notes I came across, I read the memos sent to him by the dean, and I sniffed his letters for traces of perfume.

"On a pile of papers rather dustier than the rest lay a square letter open along one edge, covered with bright stamps, postmarked — I felt a rush of adrenaline — Ethiopia!"

How incredible! First the *chammas*, and now another omen. Where was all this leading? He picked up the envelope and examined it from every angle. Strange intimacies can be fated by constraints of space, like a vacant seat on a train. Fraternation by adjunction. In his first shared office at University College in Addis Ababa, he'd known a smooth-skinned, fat, young man, as nearsighted as a mole, whose gelatinous body belied a strange history.

"At the turn of the century, my office mate's mother had been a famous, militant suffragette, leading every march in a wide-brimmed black hat, and courageously facing down the bobbies and the jibes. However, in those days before artificial insemination, what this feminist wanted, even more than the vote, was to have a child all her own.

"After nightfall, young Sylvia Pankurst would walk the docks of London searching for the father of her future child. She wanted him to be as handsome as a Roman god, as powerful as a stallion. 'With my mind and his body.' she used to say, 'he'll be the ideal person.' But you can't trifle with fate. Eventually she found the sailor of her dreams and went off happily to copulate in an English inn. Two-hundred-seventy days later, she gave birth to a chubby, pink baby who would have his father's mind and his mother's muscles. The child had become an adult hippopotamus, collapsed in his chair, writing articles on African art that no one ever read. And he grew dwarf cactus in glass pots on our common windowsill."

But these memories belonged to him alone! What right had Allan Hunger to receive correspondence from "over there"? That was his corner of the world. In a fit of jealousy, he read the letter.

Addis Ababa, November 27

Dear Professor,

I came to the capital of Ethiopia from Nairobi some ten days ago, to see how our project stood. I was most pleased to meet a female candidate whose qualifications seem, in every detail, to meet your criteria. She has some experience in the theater, speaks Italian, English, and French, and was close (too close, in my opinion) to the political changes of recent years.

The candidate, who's in a Marxist detox phase, so to speak, is religious by nature and wouldn't mind eventually leaving Ethiopia, if she were given the chance. Her parents are already living abroad.

This very afternoon, I went to the Ministry of the Interior, in a ghari driven by a maniac who almost killed me a number of times. I kept yelling "Tenish coye! Tenish coye! Slow down!" He just kept whipping his horse and trying to pass the Vespas that were coughing fumes into our faces.

Of course, at the visa office, all my inquiries were met with the standard "Ishy negheu" of the Amharic bureaucrats. But the smiles that accompanied the incantation ("Yes. Yes. Tomorrow.") indicated that a large bribe will be required. It so happens that we have a

Jacques GODBOUT

Fiat van we no longer use at the mission; it should delight the director. You'll find, herewith, an outline of what we've done so far and of the expenses that remain to be met. I know how anxious you are to find someone, dear professor, and I promise you results in the near future.

Yours etc.

Crinkling of onionskin, crocodile tears. He refolded the letter and returned it to its envelope. What exactly was Hunger looking for? A correspondent? An ally? A person who knows the theater and foreign languages? Why? Were they trying to obtain an exit visa? Under the negus, it used to be the most difficult of documents to obtain. Anyone who wanted to could enter Abyssinia, but only those whom the king of kings would allow could leave. It would have been better for him never to have seen the letter. Gregory decided to walk his thoughts through the corridors of the university. He was surprised to find himself so moved at the sight of a few simple words, long since buried in the depths of his memory. *Tenish coye.* Take it easy.

"I happened to pass a large auditorium where a black giant held two hundred students enthralled. The fellow was a basketball star, and he was lecturing on the sociological dimensions of the sport, with all doors open, so the entire university could benefit from his presentation. On another floor I noticed on the walls, here and there, blue signs proclaiming in Gothic script: 'The earth is flat.' (How many Ethiopians used to believe that? Certainly the majority had more faith in their Coptic theology than in Western science.) A little further on in the same script, but on mauve paper this time: 'Man will never walk on the moon!' I couldn't help laughing. What a great idea: to assert today in Gothic script tenets that, just yesterday, were firmly believed. Forgetting the *chammas* and Hunger's letter, I started looking for the final message. A heavy door at the end of the corridor led into a garden. I pushed it open. There it was!

"Hung between two eucalyptus, a red banner proclaimed: 'Famine will never be conquered!' Of course. It was undeniable. If the earth were flat, and if man were never going to walk on the moon, how could man overcome natural disasters? But, most astounding, who could have known I would pass that way, that I would read these slogans straight out of medieval Ethiopia? Was I still in California?

"I stood, nervous and alert, beneath the eucalyptus, which had always been our fetish wood! It grew all around the Tarafri Makonnen quarter where we had lived. Suzanne used to dry the leaves to make tea during the rainy season, and, when an army of red ants would invade the office, she would stop its advance with a freshly cut branch. The rerouted insects would cut an elegant curve on the wood floor before resolutely setting off for the house next door. The healing scent of eucalyptus would perfume the air."

Chapter 4

Closeted in the dusty university office, Gregory Francoeur drew up the outline of an investigation into happiness at forty.

"The phone on Hunger's desk rang quite frequently. At first I used to answer it, being careful to explain why I was in the office, but the callers didn't seem to care. On the fourth morning, when the phone rang for perhaps the tenth consecutive time, I snatched it up and, forgetting to speak English, snapped, 'Allô?'

" 'Professeur Hunger?' asked a firm, young voice in French. Surprised as I was, I didn't register whether it was a male or female voice.

" 'The professor is away, but I am his assistant.' I lied, wishing only to make conversation, 'What can I do for you?'

" 'Do you know if he received my letter?' The voice then identified itself: 'My name is Mary Ann Wong. I arrived from Paris this morning. I wrote ahead to let the professor know I'd be in San Francisco this week and to ask for an appointment.'

"Where the devil had I seen that name? Mary Ann

Wong. I reached for the letter postmarked Ethiopia, which was still on the desk. I checked the signature; there it was.

" 'You were in Africa?' I asked very matter-of-factly.

" 'That's right,' she answered. 'As you probably know, Doctor Hunger asked me to look into some things for him. My research has been successful. I wrote him quite a long, though necessarily rather enigmatic, letter. I mailed it in Addis Ababa.'

" 'New flower . . . ,' I muttered, 'the charming capital of the high Abyssinian plateaus.'

" 'Excuse me?' Mary Wong asked, perplexed.

" 'I said: I bet you mailed your letter at the central post office, at the foot of Churchill Street, a small brown building that also houses the Customs Office?' "

Mary Ann Wong was dumbfounded. How did this interlocutor know the place so well? Gregory was not about to explain that long ago he went there once a month to pick up Kodak slides at customs. An officer would look them over slowly, one at a time as if they might be military secrets or pornographic pictures (Suzanne lying nude on their bed), then he'd offer them up to the curiosity of a colleague. The viewing of the thirty-six slides would take all afternoon. Gregory had come to refer to these visits as his "patience therapy" and made sure always to bring a mystery novel with which to kill time and swat flies.

It was obvious that Allan Hunger, on the other hand, had never set foot in Africa. (Had he ever even set foot in his office?) Gregory could always claim that he'd become Hunger's assistant precisely because he had traveled widely and had even spent several months in Addis

Ababa. In a previous life. He explained that sometimes specific images, certain sounds or scents would trigger a flood of memories. Was it not the same for her? He sensed her amusement. The hook.

"It's true, you're right, the sound of insects varies from place to place. It's as if each city had its own song," she said. "When will I be able to see Dr. Hunger?"

"At noon tomorrow," he answered without hesitation, "if you can come to Berkeley."

She accepted at once. She knew a small restaurant called Chez Joshua, at the corner of Telegraph and Dwight Way. Would that do?

"Absolutely," Gregory answered jovially.

Then he hung up and began to worry. He had to advise his colleague. Leave a message on his desk? No good. If Hunger remained true to form, he was unlikely to come in. He got his home number from the secretary. He wanted to bring everything out into the open, except for the letter, and to apologize. He'd simply accepted a luncheon appointment for him, as a favor, that's all. Mary Ann Wong, tomorrow noon, at Joshua's. But there was no answer.

An hour later, Gregory Francoeur had to admit he'd blundered. He wasn't going to reach Allan Hunger (did he really want to?), he'd keep the story to himself, and he (the assistant!) would go to the restaurant and meet the woman who'd phoned. How old was she? Forty maybe? What if he used her as the first respondent to his questionnaire on happiness? He couldn't help hoping she was lovely and free and that she'd offer him some much needed human warmth — knees touching under the table maybe, a sparkle of complicity in the eyes, a wrinkling of the nose.

That evening he returned to Cat Haven a little

earlier than usual. He didn't even stop at Cody's to browse through the books, which he'd become accustomed to doing. He'd spent many idle hours pleasantly leafing at random through books he'd never buy. He was developing an erudition of introductions and conclusions. A practice that could serve as the basis for a course on the intellectual happiness of being superficial, he told himself.

Back at the house, he prepared a casserole of Chinese noodles, baby clams, tomatoes, and garlic. Outside the kitchen, on a window ledge, Lucifer stared at him, looking mean (or hungry). He stood with his legs stretched, his back arched, hackles raised, probably outraged that Gregory was occupying the house that was his own by satanic right. Gregory remained unmoved, having decided to serve only one cat meal a day. He wasn't about to be made a cat's patsy. Lucifer could meow till he was hoarse.

After leaving the casserole dish to soak, he felt duty bound to try Hunger again. The same shrill rings resonated in the receiver. Agitated, he hung up. Then, in spite of the time difference (California lagging three hours behind), he dialed Suzanne's number in Montreal. He had to tell someone who'd understand what was happening to him, even if it meant waking her up. He'd use the excuse that he'd found a house and wanted to give her his new address. He was told by the anonymous and distant operator that Suzanne had changed her number and that the new one was unlisted. After twenty-five years of living together it seemed an unacceptable gesture. A cruel act. As though someone had violently severed his umbilical cord.

Tears welled up in his eyes. He felt deeply humiliated; he stammered at the operator, who just kept repeating that henceforth Ms. Francoeur's number was confidential. "But I'm her husband!" he kept saying. The operator would not give in. In light of his childish anger, she was probably thinking Suzanne had been right to disconnect their relationship. *Over and out.*

"If Suzanne had come to California with me, none of this would have happened. It's not just that the circumstances would have been different: without her, I've never been able to see clearly. She has an innate gift for logic in action. She cuts through difficulties deftly, like slicing bread. Suzanne takes apart a problem the way some people peel an orange; she then places the pieces on a paper napkin and puts it back together, showing you all its subtleties. She's a rare creature, a person with whom one can passionately discuss anything and always learn something new. Even when she was only twenty, she could search among the baggage of family traditions and come up with an original answer no one had thought of. In the last few years, she's reached a level of maturity and wisdom that allows her to transform any experience into a positive gain. And that is most likely why she let me go the way a fisherman might release an undersized trout."

But, most significant, if Suzanne had come to California with him he never would have pretended to be Hunger's assistant. He never would have gotten himself mixed up in such a ridiculous situation. That night he was pacing his living room, unable to concentrate. To kill time, he turned on the tube, lit a fire in the fireplace, uncapped a beer, and sprawled out on the sofa. His legs felt tired. He lay with his hands behind his head, trying to suppress stomach spasms. He found a National Geographic presentation that took him to the heart of Africa, to the land of the Pygmies where small, naked women and tiny men wearing loincloths lead quiet lives hunting and gathering in a huge, dark forest. Life in the jungle seemed to him to be considerably simpler than life at Berkeley. The Pygmies climbed trees, wove leaves and vines, saved water in gourds. They had no telephones.

Finishing off his Japanese beer, he thought, progress being what it is, one day Pygmies will have television sets. While he watches a documentary on survival in a tropical jungle, Mr. and Mrs. Pygmy and their children will be seeing, in color and in stereo, a program featuring two Chinese cops wildly chasing notorious heroin dealers through the streets of San Francisco. Which of the two programs, he wondered, will cause the greatest cultural shock? And to whom?

Gregory remembered the terror of the day he and Suzanne, with weapons and luggage, had come down by bus from Haile Selassie airport to Addis Ababa. The bus had been forced to stop on the outskirts of the city near the Second Market. They saw three naked men, hands bound behind their backs, tied by their necks to the high branch of an oak. The men stood nonchalantly on the steel platform of the Italian truck that was blocking the road. The driver set his heavy truck in motion, honking his horn like a member of a wedding party, and the three thieves swung free, frenetically kicking their legs and shaking their shoulders, looking rather more blue than black. The minibus was then able to nudge its way through the varicolored crowd from the countryside, their arms filled with merchandise and sacks of barley. The driver brushed against the hanged men on the left, where Suzanne was seated, and on the right he greeted the two notables who had directed the proceedings, swords in hand. Seated on small arabian horses or perhaps mules, they wore lion's mane headdresses.

It was subsequently revealed, fellow humans who

will live after us, that criminals had been similarly strung up all over town. Those were the days before television allowed a single condemned person to provide an example to millions. Already badly shaken from the flight, Suzanne put her head between her knees and brought up the entire menu offered by Ethiopian Airways.

When the show ended he would gladly have followed the Pygmies down the trail on a leopard hunt. Pygmy, from the Greek *pygmaios*, is, of course, the name given to a race of dwarfs from Ethiopia.

"I wrote to Suzanne right away, before the news was picked up by the papers; I didn't want her to learn of my arrest in the media. Roenicke is going to keep it quiet as long as he can. I immediately told Suzanne that I believe the whole story to be some sort of blackmail, although no one has yet claimed a payment. I even think Roenicke is toying with me.

" 'You won't be surprised to learn,' I said to her, 'that they've accused me of torching a building in which research was being done on the use of the laser in the firing of warheads. After all these years of being pegged as a pacifist! They must have enough pictures of my face at demonstrations to mount a whole show. Anybody could have set that fire. It's just too easy to work from the motive back to the perpetrator. The same with the Cheryll Wilson business. There are three rapes a day in Berkeley, some right on the grounds of the campus. The assailants are often known. They're repeat offenders. They let them out because there's no more room in the prisons. Meanwhile, a whole new wing has been opened just for me (construction isn't even completed). It's as though they'd built it to isolate me.

" 'You can't imagine, Suzanne, how pervasive violence is in California. Insane, gratuitous, unpredictable, illogical violence flows through the streets like a form of energy. Have all the lunatics in the country conspired to spoil the dreams of Lotus Land? The rich live behind iron gates, surround themselves with uniformed guards, put seven locks on the smallest door. They're prisoners of their wealth. Others commit suicide because they've failed to attain the level of financial power they'd set for themselves. There are no social classes in California, only ladders of success and missing rungs.'

" 'And I think they're paying a high price for their lifestyles. The billions invested by the Pentagon in military and space research, in computers, nuclear technology, and the oceans is just so much blood money. Every dollar bill that goes from the engineer's pocket to the grocer's, to the wine merchant's cash drawer, or to increase the authorized Ford dealer's sales figures is a military dollar that has killed or will kill. What has currency here is not blood or money, it's power, the survival of the fittest. May the force be with you! There's racial tension, too; I feel it everywhere, especially in the public transit system. Hatred as thick as L.A. smog and everywhere someone ready to pull a knife.'

" 'I'm at an impasse,' I wrote. I asked her to get in touch with Roenicke as quickly as possible. Meanwhile, I'm writing this journal that she'll understand better than anyone else. The only crime I've committed, before God and man, was telling a ridiculous lie over the telephone. And they cut off my service."

Chapter 5

"Mary Ann Wong was not particularly surprised to see me arrive instead of the good Doctor Hunger, who she had suspected would be too busy. She introduced herself as a missionary for the Church of the Seventh Day Adventists, qualified pastor and globe-trotter for Jesus. Just my luck. She wasn't even mildly aware of the stirrings of my libido. She was at a business meeting, and she behaved accordingly. She seemed to have no doubts about anything, not the existence of Satan, or the greatness of the United States of America. Her face was strangely beautiful, a striking and successful combination of Finnish flavors and Chinese planes. A Eurasian with blue eyes and blonde hair. Nowhere in the world could she pass unnoticed; I felt everyone in the room was looking at us, women as well as men. The men speculating about the secret charms I had that they didn't.

"I had nothing but my loathsome cunning, now completely disarmed by this Christian woman with a prayer on her lips. I could see the headlines: 'Ex-minister of Catholic province in tête-à-tête with Protestant priestess.' The only hot item here was the Japanese mustard.

Concentrating on the *sushi*, I pulled my knees in under the polished wooden table and opened the conversation."

Mary Ann Wong had traveled a lot, converted many, and transported a good deal of myrrh, frankincense, gold, and pearls from free ports to other countries for the benefit of the church. She knew Allan Hunger only by reputation. She'd traveled to the five continents, but Gregory suspected she still didn't have her feet on the ground. Holding high her glass of sake, she proposed a toast to all peace-seeking enterprises, and may generous Heaven reward the old professor! Francoeur nearly choked on the hot wine. His eyes filled with tears. The missionary took this to mean he'd been touched by grace. She was beginning to like this *Québécois*.

Playing the man of the world, Francoeur asked: "Will you be in San Francisco very long?" All serious conversations begin with digressions.

"I don't know yet," she answered. "Every time I come to California I feel as if I've walked into an insane asylum. My brothers and sisters in San Francisco tell me the most incredible stories about sects and miracle therapies, computerized churches, certified cases of reincarnation. For example, did you know that only poets can come back as cats?"

"You don't like simple faiths?" asked Gregory. He was thinking that if Lucifer was a reincarnated poet, he must surely be Dante.

"The faith of the simple man, yes," answered Mary Ann Wong, "but I draw the line at regressing to the primal scream. I feel as if I'm in a huge day-care center for adults here. Therapies are changed like diapers. The care of the body takes on preternatural proportions."

"Is anything on earth more important than the self?" Gregory asked with a sardonic smile.

"Thank God," murmured the missionary, "your generous action restores my faith. But don't worry, I know it is best not to talk about it in public."

Gregory had absolutely no idea what the young woman was talking about. An *action*? Generous? Christian no doubt. He just nodded and quickly redirected the conversation. The missionary's bipolar charm was beginning to quicken his pulse. Miss North-South?

"And yet, Miss Wong, you know that the media worldwide are touting California as the precursor of future Western civilization." He gazed at her inquisitively, thinking all the while he really was quite a charmer and that he would gladly allow Mary Ann Wong to save his soul. She enveloped him in compassion. Had she no *sexuality*?!

"How can you not see," she said evenly, "that there is no human depth here, and certainly no culture? Agrobusiness, yes, show business, to be sure, tears and laboratories, but no deep sense of continuity, of the adventure of civilization. In California people seek only the solitary pleasure of success, in business as well as in human relations."

Gregory would have been happy to share his pleasure and even his failures, but Mary Ann Wong went on: "In California, only the swimming pools are deep, believe me."

"Don't forget," Francoeur couldn't help adding, "the San Andreas fault . . . "

The missionary clapped her hands, and smiling, took a sip of sake. Gregory had opened a new avenue for her.

"You're right, you're absolutely right! On the West

Coast, nature is deeper and richer than civilization. There isn't even a society here, just an agglomeration at best. Everything is built on sand, even the computer chip; it's the empire of gadgets, cut off from our universe. . . . "

"I just got here, myself." Gregory submitted by way of an excuse for not offering an opinion.

"I was born here, Mr. Francoeur."

"Ah! Here? I mean in Berkeley?"

"No," the young woman answered, "a little south of here, in Santa Barbara."

"I would never have guessed," Gregory heard himself say.

Mary Ann chuckled and lightly touched his hairy arm. Why hadn't he realized? Deep blue eyes set in the fjord depths of an oval face and those prominent cheekbones? Where else but in California could a Finn mate with a Chinese? Feeling a languorous and quite pointless warmth climb from his arm to his shoulder and the back of his neck, Gregory decided it was time to come to the heart of the matter.

"What did you think of Professor Hunger's plan?" he ventured.

"Ah, the first time was so long ago; I was skeptical, certainly," said Mary Ann Wong. "At the start the project seemed risky and pointless. Then we came to understand your objectives. And this being the eighth time, we have increasing confidence in your organization. I hope it will be easier than the last time. Did they tell you about it?"

"Of course," lied Gregory.

"When the professor asked us to act as intermediary for the transfer of a young Ethiopian woman, we had enough experience to know how to go about it. I'm not saying it was easy, but at least we didn't make any mistakes. You know that the doctor didn't want a refugee who'd made it to Cairo or Rome. He insisted on someone living in Ethiopia. We advertised that a very rich old woman, a friend of ours, wanted to appease her conscience and was, at the same time, looking for a companion for her declining years. The papers are, therefore, drawn up as adoption documents, even though the candidate is no longer a child. As usual, the twenty thousand dollars the professor deposited into the account of the Seventh Day Adventists covered all the expenses. Anything left over will go to our African missions."

"My dear colleague must have been very moved indeed by the famine to spend that kind of money! The *eighth* time? Where in the world could a respectable university professor come up with such an amount? Did he have an oil well in his backyard? And who was the old woman who had offered to adopt the Ethiopian? Mary Ann must have read his thoughts because, pointing emphatically with her chopsticks, she went on.

"You know, of course, that the aging widow is an invention, but it works every time. Probably because of the influence of Victorian literature and the recurrence of its themes in popular novels. Anyway, I've met you here today to confirm that Terounech will be arriving a week from Sunday. Is that satisfactory?"

"Terounech, if memory serves, means the 'all pure,' does it not?" That troubled him.

"Exactly," answered the missionary. "We had another prospect, the sixth child of a destitute family called Bezounech, the 'unwanted one.' But Doctor Hunger insisted that the candidate know English. So we searched among the girls who had studied at our school. Terounech comes from a good family, so to speak."

"Terounech, Bezounech — I like names that mean

something. I had a servant, once, in Addis," said Gregory, "a boy called Bellatchow."

"Which means?"

" 'Beat them up'!" he answered. "His father, the police chief of Addis Alem, was ambitious."

Their waitress, ersatz geisha, small as a doll and all rustling kimono, brought the last dish: crab flowers and avocado wrapped in dark seaweed. Francoeur felt transported, transfigured. In a paroxysm of exotic pleasure, he was almost levitating. He, who only yesterday was dragging in the muddy vicissitudes of the mundane, now sat face-to-face with a saintly woman, being secretary and front man for a saintly personage and implicated in the international traffic of kindred souls! He was discussing secret projects, savoring, with infinite delicacy, celestial foods, and fomenting revolutions of global proportions. Masticating his rice, Gregory listened contentedly to the pleasant music of the noble flights of his soul. Narcissus with chopsticks.

"How did you recruit Terounech?" he asked the Finnese.

"We didn't have far to look. She'd sought refuge in our mission at Diredawa, after some trouble with the military. At the mission she helped out with writing and with some of the accounting. But she's a child of the revolution, make no mistake about that."

"What about you," Gregory asked, "where did you learn French?"

"Six years studying in Belgium. You see what one has to go through to bring lost souls to Jesus! I have no gift for languages."

You speak admirably well." said Francoeur, because it was true and also because it would please her.

"And you don't have a Canadian accent," answered Mary Ann Wong.

He didn't react to the insult. He was too happy with the luncheon to launch into a tirade on the variations within languages.

"Thank you," he said, closing the subject. "Doctor Hunger will be there to meet his protégée."

Mary Ann Wong delivered into his hands the documents meant for Dr. Hunger: photocopies of visas, medical certificate, a letter of recommendation from the pastor of Diredawa describing the young lady's moral qualities, a transcript of her university grades in political science. Gregory asked her if she had a photograph. Mary Ann Wong was surprised he hadn't seen the one she'd sent to the professor. Gregory reminded her how absent-minded Allan Hunger could be. He wasn't taking much of a chance. Weren't all professors absentminded?

Francoeur could not resist the idea of accompanying her downtown where she was going to take the BART, a subway that goes under the bay and comes up in San Francisco.

"What took you to Ethiopia, Mr. Francoeur?" she asked as they walked down the gloriously sunny street. "Were you a Catholic missionary?"

"No, sister," Gregory laughed. "I haven't believed in God for a long time. I was searching for a new philosophy, a new way of seeing things . . . "

"All nonbelievers," answered Mary Ann Wong, "look upon life as a tourist circuit to be followed in search of truth. And yet all those countries are centuries distant from our own Christian lands! All I can say is that, in my tourist guide, Mr. Francoeur, only Christ has earned a five-star rating and only He is worth the trip.

"How old are you, Mary Ann?" Francoeur asked gently.

She shook her head in the light, as if to shake away a doubt. "Don't. Please don't ask! I'm getting close to the age of skepticism, and I'm afraid you're going to forecast some sort of crisis."

And so they picked through a basketful of acquired concepts while she showed him, street by street, ancient houses hidden behind centuries-old trees, huge wooden mansions, built, she told him, by rich merchants from San Francisco who'd been frightened by the earthquake of 1906. The architects had thought that, in the country, the walls wouldn't crumble. Today the city had caught up with them, and it was known that the main fault running out to Point Reeves in the ocean had significant branches in these hills.

"Every morning in Berkeley," she said, "conscientious housewives shake out their rugs wondering whether today is the day the world will end. And that's how, in this landscape," she concluded, thrusting out her hand, "a person can live on earth and still be dangerously close to Heaven!"

They'd arrived at University Station. He said a respectful good-bye, and she melted into the crowd, as insubstantial as an angel.

From Shattuck Street at the corner of University Avenue he could see the bay in the distance, shining like mica in the sun. On the ocean, hundreds of white triangles were crisscrossing in the wind. The sails gave the landscape a holiday air in spite of the noise, the agitation, and the heavy traffic. In the distance, Golden Gate Bridge, linking the city with the country, stood out in the fog like a musical staff.

"I was jubilant. You have to understand. I'd just made a ninety-degree turn. I have never been one to poke my nose into other people's affairs, but here I was four square in the middle of somebody else's business! Suzanne, my ex, used to tell anyone who cared to listen that in the last ten years I'd become the most petit of petit bourgeois. Totally incapable of the slightest initiative. Tossed about like a local representative casting his fate to the winds of electorate whims. And now I had provoked events. For the sheer pleasure of it. I'd invented a story to live and cast myself as its hero, come what may!

"Why, in fact, had I come to California? Certainly for more than a government-sponsored study on happiness. Was I looking for an innocence lost to political games? Mary Ann Wong had opened doors I'd thought forever closed to me. And Allan Hunger seemed a giant of historical proportions; Berkeley, a place where one could live as in a secret society. Whatever the cost, I wanted to be initiated."

Basking in the joy of his new insights, Gregory Francoeur lingered in town until evening, browsed, at a much too spicy meal in a Thai restaurant, and realized that his hemorrhoids would give him trouble for two days because he'd been too cocky to send back the offending dishes. He went into a cinema that was showing an extraordinary black-and-white film, *Stranger than Paradise*, a scathing indictment of American society, and ended the evening at Moriarty's, where an old trumpet player was blowing the blues like a fallen angel. Then he wandered home, taking streets at random, climbing as one would a ski hill, first left, then right. Reverse slalom.

"That night an alarming number of cats were

wandering the upper reaches of the town. They watched me walk by, some sitting on fences, some on all fours in front of porticos. Others followed me boldly, a few steps behind. It was like an international convention of poets. Kerouac here, John Lennon there, and on the opposite sidewalk, Prévert!"

In that neighborhood there are several University of California residences. Heating pipes from central boilers run under the streets, and when the pressure blows off through the manhole covers, foggy geysers turn the darkness into a nightmarish landscape. Some of the cats that were following him were scalded. They howled like spirits straight from hell.

"It was a carnival round of the 'lost' poets. Rimbaud chased Verlaine. Oscar Wilde mewed. Lucifer was waiting for me under a fragrant magnolia. We stared, sizing each other up. I've always loved those household pets that no one can really domesticate. They remind me of the wild cats of the negus that used to pace, like patients in an asylum common room, their concrete prisons at kilometer four, in front of the ghebi, the ancestral palace. Proud and substantial beasts, with massive muscles; symbols, in spite of themselves, of the local, mythological imperatives.

"In those days, I sometimes hurried after the day's classes to make it to the crossroads before feeding time. The keepers used to throw to the lions goats and calves whose throats they'd just cut. From the sidewalks all around, starving beggars watched the blood-smeared animals gorge themselves with satisfied grunts, tearing the flesh and swallowing greedily, their wild smell mixing with the stench of viscera and the excrements of death.

The stronger animals claimed the carcasses, and ate their share, one paw draped nonchalantly across their warm dinner; the younger lionesses waited for the second sitting.

"I was always awed at seeing them suddenly stop. Sated and happy, they would stretch and yawn widely with pleasure. I used to come close enough to the cages to touch them, but they just looked at me absently, as if I were an excess goat, hairless, odorless, and tasteless. Some of the beggars waited until the animals had shut their eyes and then tried to steal a morsel. The princes of the plains were fed seven days a week and the beggars never missed this spectacle of abundance."

Now it had become his turn to be served in a cage. Three times a day they brought him Tex-Mex food; burgers con chili prepared by assigned prisoners. Coke and coffee. He'd soon be as sleek as a lion, he thought. He put his pen down on his worktable beside an ashtray he used for paperclips and his eraser. Assuming his familiar thinking pose, Gregory touched his thumb to his nose and lay his hand along his jaw. He'd used up more than a week of the time he'd been accorded to write his journal. "Is prison writing," he wondered, "always escapist literature?"

Chapter 6

The district attorney came by in the afternoon to collect the pages he'd written. Roenicke wanted to try out a translator he'd located in San Francisco through a bookstore owner. A Parisian, he explained, who'd been drawn to the West Coast by the sexual revolution. His offices were in a tastefully renovated house on Russian Hill. Roenicke found this shuttling between Frenchmen rather amusing. Francoeur thought it ridiculous that his prose should be translated into English by a cousin from France; the one paying his ransom in words, the other being paid by the word. Everything about this misadventure smacked of the absurd.

Gregory wanted to finish his journal before he gave it to anyone. "It's in the writing that I discover the sense of things," he explained to Roenicke. "Sometimes I have to reread the whole thing before I can decide on the placement of a mere comma." Roenicke suggested they photocopy his manuscript, and Gregory relented with the proviso that he keep the original. When the district attorney had gone, Francoeur ordered a coffee from the guard, a native of southern California, and went back to his writing.

"The week following my meeting with Mary Ann Wong was particularly difficult. I made myself sick with prevaricating and hesitating, but I kept wanting to go further. What would I find if I dug deeper? What about my research? I hadn't even drawn up an outline. Should I contact Hunger? Every passing minute made our meeting more difficult. Should I meet the Ethiopian girl myself? What would I do with her? Just what kind of bizarre adoption service was the old professor running?

"Monday morning I woke up earlier than I meant to, well ahead of the alarm clock, as though I were somehow fixed in eastern time. All night my mind had raced, elaborating plans I could no longer remember. Wasted neurons. I'd forgotten to draw the *chammas*, and the room was flooded with morning light.

"Standing in front of the large, beveled mirror on the closet door, I checked myself out from every angle, as one might examine a suit. I'd been in California only a short while and already the sun had turned my face and arms the color of clover honey. The rest of my body, with its sprinkle of unruly hair, was as white as a freshly peeled apple. Fitness mania, so pervasive in this land of joggers, was beginning to get to me. I looked soft. Soon half a century, I thought, gazing affectionately at my rounded shoulders that had so often supported the weight of the world. Sadly, I wiggled my toes into the carpet, one after the other."

Gregory then got dressed to go to the university. Most of the professors, aging academics, rode to work on bicycles accompanied by faithful dogs that ran and barked everywhere, including the echoing corridors. Some left their animals to guard their offices, others brought them to class. Berkeley, reflected Francoeur, must have the densest dog population in the entire United States. *Have a nice dog.*

So the secretaries were stunned to see him arrive with a cat in tow. From the kitchen roof, old Lucifer had jumped up to the bathroom window, knocking over a spiny phallus of a cactus, and slipped into the house. At first Gregory had tried to shoo him out, but the beast knew the house like the pads of his paw. They'd spent all day Sunday getting to know each other. By sundown, Francoeur would say "come" and he'd come like a puppy; "jump" and he'd jump. The cat responded to his every command. Could he be a descendant of the great Abyssinian cats? Had he been through Rome? Could he be the son of a wild mink? Or just another missing link?

Gregory switched the conversation from Lucifer to Hunger. "That is one weird character," said one of the secretaries. In the four years she'd worked for him, she'd seen him only on the first day of each semester. He received a good deal of mail and picked it up at night. The other secretary thought him macho. For a moment the two feminist sisters discussed his libido. They finally agreed that Allan Hunger was the joke of the university but couldn't elaborate further.

In front of the urinals, a lecturer who'd overheard their conversation added that Hunger was in his early sixties, ridiculously tall, and that when he wasn't teaching he could usually be found in the main library. That would explain why they'd never met in the office. A noted Elizabethan scholar, Allan Hunger had been dedicated, for the last five years, to a detailed study of the vision of Rome in Shakespeare. He traveled a lot. "He belongs to the academic jet set," said the envious lecturer as he pulled up his fly. And he added, as he washed his hands, that Allan Hunger had discovered in London a few un-published poems by Dante. The publication of these in an annotated collection by the University Press of America had won him the respect of Western scholars. "And I," said Gregory as he gathered Lucifer into his arms, "have discovered where Dante is hiding." The perplexed lecturer smiled back vacuously.

"I could, of course, have gone straight to the library and cleared up the whole mess. But I hadn't really decided to tell him everything. And I had other fish to fry—a class to prepare, research to get underway. Continuing on to the building next door, I picked up my mail along the way, one envelope of which I recognized as being from Janvier. He was pursuing his campaign. Again, there was only a press clipping with no comment, this one from *la Presse de Montréal*. The story originated from Vacaville, a town located between Berkeley and Sacramento known primarily for its garlic ice cream. It had been filed by the American bureau of France Presse, sorted in Paris, and bounced back to Quebec. Under the picture of a bearded, long-haired, wrathful, biblical looking character carrying a case of grapefruit in a prison yard was written the following:

> Vacaville (*AFP*). Theodore Streleski, a student who spent nineteen years trying to obtain a Ph.D. and who eventually beat his professor to death with a hammer, was released yesterday after spending seven years and twenty days in various California institutions.
> Mr. Streleski, who stepped into freedom between two rows of waiting journalists, headed straight for the microphones. He stated

that if he had it to do again, he'd do exactly the same thing.

A spokesman for the Vacaville penitentiary said that the prisoner had never caused any problems, that he'd spent all his free time in the library, and that he had insisted on serving out his full term so he could work in Silicon Valley.

All through his trial the ex-student, now forty-nine years old, had insisted that killing Karel de Leew, his Stanford University mathematics professor, was a moral and logical act. The professor had no right, he claimed, to continue to pocket tuition money while refusing to grant him the degree he required to achieve his dreams.

The student had slain his professor with a 2-pound hammer.

Gregory should have stopped and deciphered Janvier's message. It contained omens, presages, and a clear warning: most obviously — professor, trial, prison. But he slipped the envelope absently into the left-hand pocket of his jacket and headed for the dusty office, mulling over the decision he had to make. Once inside, Lucifer sneezed four times, leaped onto the windowsill, and poked his nose into the fresh air.

"I was about to sit down when I noticed that the phone had been connected to an answering machine. Allan Hunger had to have been in the office over the weekend. The letter from Addis Ababa had disappeared. Had Mary Ann Wong reached him? Had he, in turn, searched my desk? The answering machine irritated me. I slumped into my chair and sat still for several moments. The initiative of the operation had been taken from me. In the distance, on the campus football field, cadet officers were sounding off a marching chant like a battle cry. What Vietnams were they preparing this time? *Have a nice war.*

"When the phone rang behind me for the first time, the machine was triggered and I finally heard Hunger's deep, firm, New York voice: 'Greetings. Activists of the world, let us unite to help Nicaragua! I'm out of the office, but if it is absolutely essential that I reach you, leave your number and the date and time of your call. This was followed by the familiar dog whistle sound signal.

"The first caller said only something like: 'This is Pete McDuff. Our good friends have agreed to meet at the appointed time.' Then he hung up. The next two or three callers didn't leave a message. Mustn't have been absolutely essential. And then, in the voice of an intimate late-night D.J. 'Do you recognize me? I love you. I got back from Japan this morning.' Tralala. 'It's Francis. There was a slight tremor last night.' She had a slight tremor in her voice. 'Don't call back. It isn't safe anymore.' I know about the voyeurs who buy *Penthouse* and about feelies who wear no underwear and sidle up to people in subway cars. But what about this auditory voyeurism? 'Activists of the world, let us unite to help Nicaragua.' "

Not long ago that message would have touched him to the core. Could Hunger be a kindred spirit? While Suzanne had classified activists as either naive, perverted, or feebleminded, he recognized only one kind and counted himself among them — those obsessed with the happiness of others. Should he act? Try to join the underground? Become militant again? Under his window students were now chanting slogans against apartheid in a mockery of the cadet officers. They were demanding that the university withdraw its investments from South Africa. IBM and Coca-Cola were taking a beating. Whoa! thought Gregory, how will I ever get them to take an interest in Quebec's nationalists who used to demonstrate against the president of the Canadian National Railway thirty years ago? Bodies never lined Dorchester Boulevard. Montreal was never Soweto. We lived a symbolic revolution, a melodrama. Today students demonstrate their solidarity with victims of tragedies. He felt it was once again time to raise his head. A new fervor seized him. *Second début.* A restorative salve for his political face.

He would gladly leave Nicaragua to Hunger if he could keep Ethiopia to himself. An image of Terounech was slowly coming together, a composite formed of memories of Suzanne and of the smiles of prostitutes along Saint-Georges Square soliciting passersby through red curtains partially open onto their pleasure haunts. Sometimes she wore a traditional *chamma*, other times he dressed her in the sweater, calf-length skirt, and colored sneakers of a college student.

If Terounech were to come and share his somber castle, would the good people of Elmwood accept a black girl in their neighborhood? What were the terms of the lease? The neighbors would probably gossip, but would they try to apply pressure? What about those self-appointed civilian police, the vigilantes, who patrol the streets? And the nosey parkers behind their curtains? Would Terounech even agree to come with him in the first place?

"It was eleven o'clock in the morning, and I hadn't

yet written the opening line of my first lecture. I wouldn't be good for anything until I'd made a decision. Should I call Mary Ann Wong? Maybe it would just arouse her suspicions if she hadn't made any further attempts to reach the professor. I decided to check out the man himself at the library. I didn't want to speak to him so much as to size him up. When I left, I closed the door behind me, leaving Lucifer asleep in the office."

In each classroom a teacher was holding forth in a loud voice in front of a group of students whose spines were twisted into so many impossible positions on their uncomfortable chairs. Outside, in the February sunlight, sycamores plastered with slogans reached their warty branches into a sky as deep blue as the bottom of a swimming pool. Gregory followed a path up to a building in the shadow of the campanile that overlooked the campus and steeped it in European nostalgia. The library, divided into sections, spread out into various annexes. The main room was completely undistinguished: soft lights, straight chairs, wooden tables, functional organization. A librarian asked to see Gregory's card, then pointed out a busy-looking Allan Hunger, sitting at one of the long tables at the back of the room, surrounded by open books spread in a circle, like the foundations of an igloo.

The man looked like a sad clown. A bright red, gold-flecked motorcycle helmet lay at his feet, and his wavy, gray hair grew over the collar of his navy blue shirt. He wore a tweed jacket and the mandatory tie that distinguished professors from the students, who were allowed to wear T-shirts, jeans, shorts, and worse. His face was rather round, his complexion olive, and his eyebrows thick and unruly. Francoeur could not make out his eyes behind small, rectangular glasses. Hunger had the look of a sedentary man, with his rounded shoulders and small, delicate hands. A single, deep line furrowed his brow.

Gregory sat a few tables away to watch his man. Periodically a student would enter the room, blink, get his bearings, and deliver a document to the professor. Sometimes the professor would take an envelope from the black backpack at his feet and give it to the student, then, without saying a word, he'd return to his work. He seemed to be drawing up an endless list of words, some of which he would occasionally look up in a dictionary. Only once did their eyes meet, but Allan Hunger appeared to be nearsighted and unable to see him clearly. Gregory was startled by the noonday chimes. He withdrew as the bell ringer in the adjacent quad struck the hardwood keyboard with his gloved fists. "I'll write to him," he thought, "it'll be easier than going over and confessing my indiscretion to him in a whisper. In fact, we may never speak. Really, we have nothing to say to each other. I just have to clarify one point." Gregory left on tiptoe, more timidly than he would have thought.

"Meanwhile, during my absence, Lucifer had awakened in the throes of a claustrophobic panic. He'd attacked, tooth and nail, a few of the massive volumes of the *Grand dictionnaire universel du XIX siècle*, put out by Pierre Larousse, which were kept right next to the window. The bindings of these masterworks were in shreds. It would henceforth be impossible to tell the eleventh volume (*NEM-OZ*) from the ninth (*H-K*). I tried to repair the worst damage with Scotch Tape. Dad would have been pleased. He had taught me respect for dictionaries, and particularly for alphabetical order. My childhood home, from the front door to the back, from the basement to the attic, had polished copper labels on every drawer and cupboard door. 'That way nothing is lost,' Dad used to say. 'And nothing is created,' I could have added. I owed my sense of order to Dad and a mania for cleanliness to my mother.

"That's why the previous day, Sunday, I had spent several hours putting to rights the decor of Cat Haven. I'd searched both garage and attic for objects that would suggest a familiar Ethiopia, a domesticated Africa. I turned up pictures of wild animals, painted pottery, colorful fabrics, woven baskets with strands of red and black, sheathed machetes, a huge hippopotamus skin shield, a certificate attesting to the fact that the owner had, on one of his voyages, scaled the fifty-eight hundred meters of Uhuru Peak on Mount Kilimanjaro. I hung the document, signed by the superintendent of parks for Tanzania, in the kitchen, then cleaned the other articles and disposed them carefully throughout the house. The effect was quite appealing.

"Seated on the couch over which I'd hung scenes of a leopard hunt, I tried to explain to Lucifer why Suzanne had left me to my own devices. I told him about the limits of monogamy in a society where life expectancy had reached a level such that marriages were dying of boredom. As long as Janvier had lived at home, I explained to the cat who was all ears, Suzanne and I didn't think anything was wrong. But once the nest was empty, it came on us in a rush.

"That's exactly when I should have been most attentive to her, but I was completely preoccupied with myself. Like an egg, I wanted only to be incubated and coddled. I had gone into politics. The more I enjoyed crowd baths, the less frequently I showered with my wife. She was letting me out the back door because I'd exchanged the thrill of her sweet murmurings for the excitement of applause."

Sitting in front of a sandwich and coffee, with Lucifer lying at his feet, Gregory Francoeur set to work. "Dear Allan Hunger: I am your new office mate." He threw twenty drafts into the waste basket. How could he explain in two pages that he felt like a chrysalis? That from the depths of his cocoon he too heard the universe cry out. That he wanted to get outside himself, give of himself, transform himself, leave his old self behind. That he had used Terounech's arrival as a means of becoming involved. Indeed: that Terounech was keeping an appointment fated from the beginning of time. He didn't want to lose her now that he knew her. He was prepared to help in any way possible. Was he needed in Nicaragua? He was ready to volunteer his services anywhere in the world.

But every time he read a draft, he could hear Suzanne calling him back to her reality: "If you ever leave your cocoon, it'll only be to flit once again like a butterfly." Hands thrust in his pockets, he stood for a long moment in front of the open window, trying to conjure up the scent of eucalyptus. Nostalgia.

Chapter 7

In an attempt to forget that he either hadn't known how or hadn't wanted to face his opponent, Gregory spent long hours dealing with the logistics of framing his research into the concept of happiness.

He didn't want to make it another poll on consummer habits and/or the pleasures of driving a Mercedes. Late in the afternoon, when he'd completed his lecture notes for the next day, he returned to Cat Haven and went to bed early. He didn't particularly like himself in the role of retired activist, and he had trouble getting to sleep.

"At about three o'clock in the morning, I heard the phone ring at the top of the stairs. With difficulty I managed to bring myself around enough to get up. I was startled by the second ring. In the middle of the night, it could only be bad news. Then I thought that perhaps Suzanne hadn't remembered the three-hour time difference. Forgetting that she didn't even have my number, I figured out, watch in hand, that it would be six o'clock in Montreal. That was just like my wife. So when I picked up the receiver, I was surprised to hear a voice that was drier and breathier than hers, with a Germano-American accent. I identified myself and asked who it was.

" 'Thank you for answering at this late hour, Mr. Francoeur. My name is Elizabeth and I belong to the Sanctuary movement,' the strange voice explained in English. (I grunted.) 'I'm calling on behalf of sister Mary Ann. She left us your name. I got your number from directory assistance.'

"It seemed plausible. When I'd rented the house I'd taken over the telephone account, and my name must have replaced the former occupant's.

" 'This is my first call. I'm deeply grateful to the Adventist mission for waking me at three A.M. to welcome me to California. Is this a religious observance of yours?'

" 'Mr. Francoeur, Mary Ann warned me about your wicked sense of humor.' answered Elizabeth, the stranger.

" 'And where is Miss Wong at this ungodly hour?' I inquired somewhat peevishly.

" 'In Boston, for the time being. That's why I have taken this upon myself. We have a difficult little problem, Mr. Francoeur, and tonight you're the only one who can help us.'

" 'I'm listening,' I said. My heart was racing. Was this the long-awaited sign?

" 'You're familiar with the Sanctuary movement?' she asked.

" 'Yes,' I answered.

"I'd read in the *New York Times* that the American government was investigating certain Protestant ministers who'd given shelter to some two thousand political refugees. I thought they were very brave. Several had been heavily fined and others had ended up in jail.

" 'I'm speaking freely for two reasons, Mr. Francoeur. First, I don't think the authorities have bugged your phone yet. You just got here. And Mary Ann told me you were Professor Hunger's new assistant. We all know and love the professor. I hope you'll give him our best regards; we hardly ever see him.'

" 'Yes, of course.' I winced.

" 'Mr. Francoeur, one of our members was in a serious accident tonight and you're the only person who can take his place. Can we count on you?'

"The stairway window was a dark blank, much like my mind. I was about to be swept up by events. A moth in the night.

" 'Let's synchronize, it's three-oh-seven,' said the voice.

" 'Done, what next?' I asked.

" 'You'll get dressed, go out the back door, and skirt the north wall of the house to the sidewalk. If it's all clear, head for the underground parking garage under the Presbyterian church at the bottom of your street.'

"I had noticed a long building on concrete pilings designed somewhat like a ship and built with upright boards in a modern spiritual style. I described it.

" 'That's it,' Elizabeth answered. 'You'll find a gray Toyota in the garage; the keys are behind the left rear wheel. I should tell you there are two men lying in the trunk. Don't worry, we've punched holes so they can breathe.'

" 'Who are they?'

" 'Members of the Farabundo Revolutionary Front wanted by American Immigration for taking part in the demonstration yesterday in front of Sproul Hall. Were you there?'

" 'No, I couldn't make it.' "

" 'Anyway, you know it was Dr. Hunger's idea that we hold daily strategy sessions to denounce apartheid, U.S. aggression in South America, and so on.'

"I was getting it. Activists of all countries! Hunger was not satisfied with adopting Ethiopians in collusion with Christian missionaries, he was campus coordinator for all political struggles. I could see the paper banners students prepared every morning and stuck to buildings with Scotch Tape so as not to damage the walls. Short-haired, image-conscious preppies with clean hands. Orderly demonstrations. Their predecessors, those of the heroic Vietnam era, would have trouble recognizing their children.

" 'What exactly do you want from me?' I asked. 'And why me?'

" 'Because, Mr. Francoeur, they're not on to you yet.' She said it as if she were addressing a child. 'We want you to drive the refugees. Those two men are very important to the movement. They're in the States right now to raise money. Frankly, without your help, their safety might be in serious jeopardy.'

" 'Which means?'

" 'Which means that if these people are caught by Immigration and deported, there's a good chance they'll be killed.'

" 'Where do I have to drive them?' Time was of the essence, and I wasn't going to fool around. When you've got a leading part in the big adventure, you can't be playing Solomon.

" 'You'll find a map on the dashboard. The route is marked out in yellow. Eventually you'll come to the end of a secondary road, then down to the end of a dirt road. Don't worry, the car's never been used to transport illegals before. You have to get there before sunup. We won't be far behind you.'

" 'I appreciate your confidence.' I said.

" 'God bless you and thank you.'

"The receiver went dead. Elizabeth had hung up. What kind of bad movie was I in? Is this what that gossip columnist was talking about?"

Gregory dressed quickly, pulled on a dark wind-breaker, went into the kitchen, and put on water for a quick instant coffee while he gathered his keys and papers. When he opened the door, Lucifer followed him out. The two of them hurried quietly along the sidewalk which had been buckled intermittently by tenacious roots. The underground lot glowed dimly under grate-covered neon lights. The Toyota was parked near the exit, at some distance from the other presumably clerical vehicles. He got the key from its hiding place, opened the door, allowed Lucifer to jump in, and started up the engine. It purred like a kitten. He threw the car into gear, and when he moved into the street, he called out "Hombre!" in greeting to his passengers. He heard friendly grunts from the trunk.

He tooled down College, found Ashby, took Highway 13 by way of Walnut Creek. The route wound toward Fairfield via the Concord Hills. Even in the dead of night, the expressway was not deserted. Several semis roared past him. He checked his rearview mirror. It didn't look as if he was being followed. In fact, at this time of the morning, he seemed to be the only one driving within the speed limit. Taking no chances, he stuck to the inside lane. He turned on the radio, and with his uncomfortable passengers in mind, he looked unsuccessfully for a station that played pleasant music, all the while keeping his eyes on the roadsigns from which glowed the names of the exits.

An hour and twenty minutes later, Gregory turned the Toyota off the six-lane expressway and onto a narrow side road. Beyond the shoulder on either side the headlights revealed cloud-shaped bushes. Fairfield was behind him and to his left, and farmland stretched as far as he could see. He was looking for the junction where, according to his instructions, two white churches faced each other from opposite sides of the road. Only a helicopter could have followed him through these fields. Gregory glanced anxiously up at the sky, which was beginning to lighten. The churches were smaller than he'd expected. In one of them, the faithful, basking in candlelight, sang of God's glory and man's suffering. He parked the Toyota beside the chapel, opened the trunk, and found the two men all curled up. He helped them out. They were neither broad nor tall. He thought them handsome and serene, and he shook their hands effusively. The sound of the insects mingled with the music from the choir.

"We embraced and kissed one another on the cheeks, as it is customary for these men to do. It's not my style, but the poignancy of the moment, the setting, the music, the time, my exhaustion, and the sense of a good job well done brought tears to my eyes. I knew we'd never cross paths again. They slipped, as planned, into the lighted chapel."

On the drive back the morning sun shone on a distant harbor where hundreds of warships, abandoned since 1946 by the look of them, were slowly rotting away. Fantastic Pacific vision! "All the cries and shocks and smells of naval combat those steel ghosts must hold!" imagined Francoeur. Aircraft carriers lay like monstrous parking lots amid a jumble of iron and brass and steel.

"The road curved and the gray carcasses of the destroyers disappeared behind purple hills. Lucifer had curled up on a folded blanket and was looking out the back window at the ever increasing parade of suburbanites driving into San Francisco, headlights blazing.

"I hadn't seen such a play of light on clouds and the horizon since I'd watched the sun rise on the African plain! Leopard hunting expeditions also began in the dark. After four hours of driving, the Land Rover was bumping its way along a dusty track, followed by the rocking Volkswagons. We were feeling our way blindly among the acacia trees.

"Five A.M., November. The first rays are touching the clouds and turning them blood red. When our caravan arrived the night before, we had cautiously pitched the tents in a semicircle and turned the vehicles to face the track. Once we'd turned off the engines, we had stayed inside for several minutes as the dust settled in the beams of the headlights. Then everything had become a pulsing calm. We were all uneasy as we unpacked our supplies. The braver ones shone their flashlights into the bush from which wild cries rose in flurries. But all we saw were twisted tree trunks, emptiness, and occasionally a pair of yellow eyes that would glow at us, then disappear. We made a fire, drank cognac from the bottle, and ate cream cheese and crackers. We went to bed, vowing, all of us, hunters, women, and children, to get up early for a morning expedition.

"Of course I was the only one to get up early. Good scout, always right there for the call. Coffee. Toast burned over the embers. At the break of the day, the landscape retains none of the night's menace. By accident we have pitched camp on an elevation. In the distance a few straw huts dot the terrain. I grab the Mauser, gripping the polished wood, thumb on the safety catch, and head toward a hillock to the left. I try to be quiet so as not to disturb even the insects. I take five steps. I stop. I listen. A breath of wind picks up. I count five more steps. A guinea fowl flies from one tree to another with a staccato beating of wings. I freeze for a moment. Suzanne must still be asleep, groggy from the cognac like the rest of them. I take almost an hour to walk around the hill.

"The trees are closer together at the foot of the hill. Then, all of a sudden, a golden clearing. Three gazelles are grazing peacefully. I'm downwind. Trembling, I shoulder my weapon. I can barely see I'm so nervous. My heart is beating wildly. I try to take deep breaths. Will I bring down the one on the left, the biggest one, or the nearest one first? Slowly I calm myself until I'm just as still as my prey who haven't yet seen or gotten wind of me, and who continue to graze on the dewy grass as peaceful as goats in a paddock. Then, the explosion, four quick shots. One shell remains in the chamber.

"Two gazelles go down, whimpering. A third bounds off. Is it hit? I run after it, but it's no use. How will I get these trophies and all this meat back to camp? How will I find them again? I hang my blue checked shirt on a branch and start running back toward camp, leaving a handkerchief on a thorn here, a sock on a branch there. When I finally get back to camp, they're all up sipping coffee. I'm in my underwear beaming like a successful pigmy hunter. They give me a hearty ovation. I get an erection."

It was nearly seven when he returned the Toyota

to the garage where he'd taken it. The cat jumped deftly down and headed off to hunt birds. Francoeur walked back to Cat Haven like an automaton. He picked up a newspaper wrapped in lavender plastic which had been thrown on the doorstep, and tripped up to bed. His first class was at half past ten.

Chapter 8

That Wednesday, prosecutor Roenicke had a note delivered which Gregory had been expecting for days. The typed memo announced that Suzanne was to arrive in San Francisco at the end of the week. She was bringing a lawyer from Quebec to take over his defense. The guard who delivered the note was astounded by the reams of yellow paper Gregory had blackened with his neat writing.

"You writing a novel?" he asked. He couldn't understand why so many pages would be needed just to clear up what to him was a simple moralities case. He blinked his eyes as he spoke: he liked girls too but favored brothels over assault. How did the *French rapist* like them? Young, sweet asses, firm, colored, tender, trim, or tanned? Couldn't he find what he needed on campus?

Gregory explained that he'd left the initiating of sunshine coeds to cornflakes heroes and orange juice athletes. The guard looked at him with a skeptical smile. Francoeur explained that the day of intimacies with coed kittens was gone. Professors now had to interview students with their office doors wide open. A representative of the sexual harassment committee carefully investigated every complaint brought by any young woman who felt her virtue had been compromised or threatened. "If Don Juan were alive today, he'd be dying of paranoia," Gregory added.

The guard took another tack. "It's perverts like you who haven't got the balls to go all the way that end up torching buildings." Less than a hundred years ago, if it had been left up to characters like this guy, Francoeur would have been lynched with no further ado. A posse of prospectors or cowboys would have strung him up from the nearest oak. From suspicion to rope, Western justice was often expeditious. Before retiring to the saloon, the crowd would have applauded both hangmen and victim. I would have died with an erection, thought Gregory.

The guard left with a shrug. He chose to go smoke a cigar in his cubicle rather than listen to stupid theories about writing and sexuality. He would have liked best of all to take his prisoner down to the yard and watch the interinstitution baseball game. But with Suzanne coming, Francoeur had to get as much of his journal done as he could.

"When I got back from my trip to Fairfield in the Toyota, I slept for a couple hours, then I woke up with a start. Shortly thereafter, my eyes still heavy with sleep, I found myself in front of my students. They were all well rested, healthy, tanned, and beautiful. I would have liked to tell them about my adventures of the previous night to build up my credibility. But underground politics are not like election campaigns. They probably thought I was hung over, and there was nothing I could do about it. The Asian students were particularly unforgiving, in spite of all my efforts. What could I say? When I haven't had enough sleep, my blood just doesn't seem to flow fast enough. Dull noises murmured in my ears. My voice came out in a flat monotone. They stared at me as they might at their PC screens or at a pale, cathodic picture tube starved of power. I was moving like a figure in an outdated computer game, a television shadow. The girls were listening politely enough, although some seemed to be considering the possibility that I might be a gigolo just back from a wild night in some Spanish dive.

"I was passionately explaining the difference between the French and the English view of politics, the different ways in which we lie about the same things in Canada's two official languages. The examples I was providing were hilarious. Not one question. Not a single comment. Not a smile. They left the room with complete indifference, as though I'd just dissected a rat. I had not been a hit. I'd have to change my style if I wanted to play to a full house. I didn't want my days as a lecturer to be cut short by a blow to the head with a hammer. My tongue was dry and my mouth tasted bitter. *Have a nice sleep.*"

When they'd all left, Francoeur perused the computerized class list. He wondered how many would show up next time. What could he possibly talk about that would capture their interest? How long could he go on saving the world at night and still get his work done during the day? Could he have landed on the wrong planet altogether? Exhausted by his poor performance and his sleepless night, Gregory Francoeur returned to Cat Haven earlier than usual. He was dead on his feet. Maritain was running an infernally loud power mower over his motley lawn. When he saw Gregory he ran over to congratulate him on his new acquisition.

"What acquisition?" Although he certainly didn't

feel like chatting, Francoeur had to know what the caretaker was so excited about.

"The Toyota! I saw you go out for a spin this morning!" said Maritain.

Gregory was suddenly wide awake, and he felt a rising anger. He hated being spied on. His face went crimson.

Sensing the need for an explanation, Maritain continued quickly. "I can't sleep at night," he said, "I often get up and wander around the neighborhood. I borrow a paper from someone's doorstep, read it under a lamppost and return it before anyone's missed it. (I am on top of the news before anybody else.) This morning I saw you driving along College Street toward the expressway."

Gregory realized he'd have to come up with a plausible story. Maritain could be an FBI informer. Or a CIA agent. He lied as best he could:

"Yes, it's too bad though, I decided not to buy it. It had a nasty tendency to pull to the left. I wanted to try it out, and since the owner uses it for his work, I had to do it at night."

Seeing that his story was taking, Francoeur decided to push it a little further.

"Maybe you could help me find a used car? I don't know much about cars and even less about the market out here."

"Of course!" Maritain was delighted. The thing he liked most in the world was to help people out and maybe pick up a little cash for his trouble. He'd check for deals. Francoeur thanked him and went in the back door as the caretaker finished up his gardening chores. He was famished, so he took a can of fruit from the shelf. Eating right from the tin, he forked out the biggest pieces, drank the sickly sweet syrup, careful of the serrated edge, and wiped his mouth with the back of his hand. Through the window he could see Maritain speaking to Lucifer. A wave of exhaustion washed over him. He drew the curtains, turned on the television, and dropped onto the couch. He fell asleep, sweating profusely, as America convulsed to the pleasure of guessing the price of a prospective prize. Electronic orgasm.

In his deep sleep he could hear cries, gun shots, music, but he'd fallen so far under that he couldn't heave himself into semiconsciousness for more than a second at a time. At about ten o'clock there was a knock at the door. Thinking the sound was coming from the TV, Francoeur took a while to answer. The caretaker had returned, and he was waving a car trade magazine in which he'd jotted notes, circled a price, and underlined a number. Francoeur was surprised at the age of the cars. Models that in Quebec had long since rusted out and been retired to junkyard scrap heaps were selling here, with pedigrees, for fabulous prices! Maritain was promoting a model very sought after on the coast, a twelve-year-old Beetle that could be Gregory's for a mere fifteen hundred dollars. It was awaiting his pleasure across the street. How could he resist?

"My first car, the first car I ever owned in my life, was a bluish gray Volkswagon I bought in Ethiopia. The back window was so small it looked like the window of a diving suit. It used to be said that the Beetle was so well made that if it fell into the water it would float high and dry like a bar of Ivory soap. To give it a classier look, I had painted in whitewalls with rubber paint, and every Sunday evening after a drive to Mount Entono or out to Adama, I'd take out the paint and touch them up. In Adama a group of us foreign teachers used to get together on the stone terrace of the only hotel and drink warm beer, which we tried to defend from hordes of hairy flies. Natives would come to check us out. Assailed by noisy flies, they'd stand a few yards off, leaning gracefully on their shepherds' staffs. With their eyes half-closed by glaucoma, they seemed aloof and indifferent.

"The later it got, the larger the crowd of curious and the more they closed in on the terrace. The heavy air became scented with the sweet smell of the rancid butter they used in their hair. Some of the white drinkers became nervous. They called out, exhorting the waiters with promises of generous *baksheeshes* to chase off the herdsmen. The waiters did nothing at all. They had little respect for any of us. We were the first race that God had removed too soon and too pale from his solar oven.

"They believed that the Creator had tried again, and that this time He'd waited too long. The second race had come out overbaked and blackened. The first batch, they used to say, He'd discarded in Europe, the second, in the heart of Africa; then he'd tried again. To this race, His masterpiece, neither under- nor overcooked, done to the beautiful color of a gazelle's coat, he'd given Life and the land of Ethiopia.

"From the rocky path that bordered the hotel, men of the race done to a turn looked at us quizzically. They wondered what we had to offer their civilization, why the negus, their beloved emperor, the king of kings, descendant of Balkis and of Solomon, had invited us to these high plateaus. To drink beer? To sit idly all day in small chairs?

"One Sunday, Suzanne pointed out that the archaeological site where the oldest hominids had been discovered was in the Omo valley, just a few hours from the Adama Hotel. 'No wonder these poor wretches are so primitive,' a drunk had replied. Suzanne had leaped up, poured her beer over his head, and exhorted the flies to make a meal of him! Then she'd knocked him to the ground, where he rolled around trying to protect himself and apologizing profusely. The herders had enjoyed this performance immensely. We drove back to Addis Ababa in silence. Before dinner I took some time touching up the whitewalls of my first Beetle."

The California Beetle sitting in front of the door seemed only to be awaiting the touch of a wand to transform itself into a pumpkin. It had been hand-painted by a graphic arts student and the interior had been redone by a gay, obdurate hippy in Day-Glo tones of pink and green. Evidently the fenders had taken some hard knocks in parking lots and rallies.

"I asked to take it for a spin right away. It seems I was acquiring an affinity for nocturnal living! Maritain sat in the suicide seat, and we took off, driving north down the highway that borders the bay. The motor purred at high speed, the brakes were responsive, headlights and signals worked, and even the radio played energetically. We turned around in Albany and decided to head back to Berkeley. The insomniac caretaker suggested I buy the car before midnight. Cinderella was reluctant. 'This wagon is gold,' he said. Expensive but righteous. A great vintage: 1972! However, I had to act fast. I had to decide now, even as we hurtled down the highway.
    " 'Did I get you a great house?' he asked.
    " 'I even like the cats,' I admitted.
    " 'So trust me. Let's go see the man right now!'
    " 'Will he take a check?'
    " 'I'll personally guarantee it.'

He was so insistent I had little choice. I wondered how much Maritain was making on this deal. I tried one last maneuver.

"'Won't he be asleep?'

"'He's crashing in People's Park. If he is sleeping, it'll be easy enough to wake him up.'"

Since the political confrontations of the sixties, People's Park has become such a famous place that neither the university, which owns the property, nor the municipality in whose jurisdiction it is, nor the police authorities have dared touch it. Much of it is overgrown. Every Sunday citizens plant trees or bushes, but they have trouble taking root in the high grass. The park is strewn with tin cans and garbage, and it looks more like a vacant lot than a political project. But Berkeley is probably the most leftist community in the United States, certainly where individual rights are concerned. The place is dotted with churches. The town council has even voted a strict ordinance closing the urban area's airspace to military planes carrying nuclear weapons. Copies of the resolution were formally sent to Moscow and Washington. A city sacred to all the Allan Hungers of the world!

At night People's Park is inhabited by vagabonds, musicians in rags, gentle, demented bag ladies, ancient victims of one-way acid trips, red-headed giants, and black bohemians gathered around wood fires burning in old oil drums. Maritain had Gregory leave the car on Haste Street, then he led him into the bushes to meet the Beetle's owner. They found him sheltered from wind and smoke in a cardboard lean-to next to a concrete podium where a boy was singing in Spanish and playing flamenco tunes on the guitar.

"I was surprised to recognize the big fellow. I'd often seen him, wearing a black suit and striped tie, preaching the imminence of Armageddon in front of the university gates, and I'd always thought he was a Protestant evangelist. Every day at noon he took up his position at Sather Gate in the company of a tiny old crone whose greatest pleasure seemed to be releasing soap bubbles into the azure sky. Often students would bait him, and his sermon would degenerate into ribald banter. 'The Lord said: Repent before it's too late!' the preacher would cry. 'The Lord said: Screw everybody you can before it's too late!' the evangelized would reply.

"In the darkness of People's Park, the pastor seemed calm and well rested. Maritain told him I was interested in buying his car if he still wanted to sell it. Turning toward me, he asked, 'Will you take good care of her?' Then, frowning, he added: 'What do you do?' I told him I was a seeker after truth and that the Beetle might put me on the road to fulfillment.

" 'This guy's crazy,' the pastor observed. The caretaker looked at me with admiration.

" 'Aren't we all,' he answered.

"I asked if the car had been baptized. If there was a name it answered to. The pastor frowned again. It was increasingly damp in the bushes, and we were getting waves of uric stench from a nearby latrine. I wanted to move closer to the fire.

" 'Apocalypse! That's what she's called, and the price is fifteen hundred bucks!'

"Maritain swore he could vouch for my signature, and I wrote out the check by the light of the fire, leaning the checkbook against the caretaker's back.

" 'Aristotle!' the pastor shouted over our heads, 'I've sold Apocalypse!'

" 'Who to?' The young bard had stopped playing and was heading toward us.

" 'To this gentleman. How about that?'

"Aristotle watched with incredulity while I handed the check to the pastor, and then, before I could even raise my arms to protect myself, he hit me over the head with his guitar. Then he hit me again on the shoulder. I saw Maritain lunge at him just as a last whack to my head laid me out in the field. I heard some yelling; I felt very cold; I passed out.

" 'An episode,' the cop who'd driven the caretaker and me to the hospital in a patrol car was explaining. 'It's in their genes. We've discussed it with the mayor. They're gentle, calm, courteous, then, all of a sudden, they attack. Sometimes they kill. You can't really blame them. But it does present a bit of a security problem.'

" 'Feeling better?' inquired Maritain. 'We should have been more careful. These guys are turfed out by psychiatrists who want to reintegrate all mental patients into the community. Apparently Aristotle had an unreasonable attachment to Apocalypse.'

" 'It's an example of erratic behavior brought on by chemical processes,' the young cop, who reminded me of Janvier, was expounding. 'An expert explained the whole thing to us in class the other day. For instance: if my wife looks at me a certain way, acids irritate my neurons and I react. Only my upbringing and my willpower keep me from hitting her. All desires can be traced to a handful of phosphorus. All pleasures to neurochemical reactions. That's just the way it is.'

"Lying on a hospital gurney, my shirt stained with blood, I asked in a weak voice: 'Aren't you going to arrest him?'

" 'What good would it do?' the officer argued.

'They'd only let him out again in three days. We calmed him down.'

"Maritain added warmly, 'Anyway, the important thing is you're alive.'

"Then he gave me the keys and the ownership papers to Apocalypse. *Have a nice car.*

" 'What am I doing now?'

" 'She's all yours. You even paid for her with your own blood. I'll help you work out the registration tomorrow. They'll be keeping you here till you're back in fighting form.'

" 'I'll drive you home,' offered the cop, leading Maritain by the arm as if he were the victim.

"They left me lying on a high gurney in the deserted emergency room of a large hospital. A nurse brought me coffee. I would never again be surprised by even the most outrageous items in the local press. I've always had a great lust for life. And I'd made it through the murderous scene with the guitarist. That was a good sign. At about three o'clock, after they'd x-rayed my skull and shoulders and found everything intact, I was released. At the time of night when lions come down to the watering hole and when missionaries transport illegals, an intern cleaned my wounds, put eight stitches in the back of my scalp, and covered it with a light gauze bandage so the air could get at it. He had looked at me the way a craftsman might admire a successful vase.

"I was invited to spend the rest of the night in a hospital bed for three hundred dollars. The Apocalypse had already cut into my savings. I found myself on the street in a vicious rainstorm, an unexpected, freezing winter downpour that had me soaked to the bone in seconds. But for the quality of the sutures, my brain would have been swamped. *Have a nice flu.*

"I ran for the shelter of some red pines by the road-side. Having just had my scalp pulled back together, I really had no desire to return with terminal pneumonia. Not a single cab cruised by. What is a man profited if he shall gain the whole world and lose his own car? Walking in a wind as wet as a dog's nose, I headed back to the Apocalypse. Raindrops bounced off the roadway; which shone silver under the streetlamps."

After all the trauma he'd been through, Gregory found himself overwhelmed by a sudden urge for hot tor-tillas, fresh guacamole, and Mexican beer. Salivating, he left the Apocalypse by the side of the road and entered a restaurant with brown tables, whose sole occupant was a diminutive cook. He sat by the window and ordered. He would be the last patron this night. A flowering prune in front of the restaurant announced the end of winter. (He was noshing on natchos dunked in tomato puree.) In Montreal, dandelions herald the spring; in Abyssinia it's the *maskal*, a yellow daisy young girls weave into chains and wear around their heads.

Raising his eyes as he drank, Francoeur noticed a sign on a closed restaurant across Telegraph Street: the Blue Nile. By squinting, he could almost make out, what else? — "Ethiopian cuisine." Gregory couldn't believe it. He asked the cook, who was busying himself in front of the ovens, whether he'd read it correctly. The Mexican told him that on the same street, in the short distance be-tween Berkeley and Oakland, the Blue Nile was only one of four Ethiopian restaurants in competition for the spicy food trade. The Sheba, just up the street, had two stars in the *Definitive Guide to the Bay Area's Best*. White peb-bles. Hansel and Gretel revisited.

The cook brought him his enchiladas, took off his

chef's hat, and sat down in front of Gregory, hands tucked under his buttocks.

"You been in an accident?" he asked.

"An incident," answered Gregory, "but it's over now." His shirt had dried. The spicy food had perked him right up.

"You heard the news today?" the man asked him. "You interested in Ethiopia?"

"It's more like Ethiopia's interested in me. Why? What're you getting at?"

"All right, let's see how good you are," he said, pointing to the two stars the Sheba had earned. "For fifty thousand dollars."

"What am I guessing?" asked Francoeur.

"What the stars have to do with the news of the day."

"Star wars?" suggested Gregory.

"Wrong; guess again." The old cook was having a grand time. "It has to do with politics."

"The Star of David!" Francoeur shouted.

"Bang on!" (The Mexican slapped his thighs.) "It said on the news tonight that over the last two months Israel has illegally smuggled out, through the Sudan, twelve thousand starving Ethiopian Falashas!"

Gregory reflected that Allan Hunger was in serious company and that the Mexican might soon have more competition: Famine Café, Destitution Diner.

Overjoyed at having found someone to talk to, the sententious, politicized cook went on:

"That very act proves that Zionists take care of their own wherever they are! Henceforth, the Ethiopians from Gore, refugees from Budapest, survivors of the Warsaw ghetto and merchants from Marrakesh can all rub shoulders at the Wailing Wall."

In the market in Addis Ababa, Francoeur had met Falashas, who'd come down to the capital to sell jewelry and Ge'ez manuscripts. Some, believing themselves to be the last surviving tribe of Israel, had converted to Christianity or Islam. Black Jews of misfortune.

Noticing for the first time that his complexion was rather light, Francoeur asked the cook: "You're not Mexican, are you?"

"Of course not. I was born in Baghdad of Jewish parents. But in this place, to earn a living, you have to play a role. I chose this one thirty-five years ago. What's yours?"

Francoeur realized that if he was ever going to get any sleep that night, it was time to pay the bill. Rain was still falling, and the Apocalypse was shining in the street. He climbed behind the wheel and dozed off before he'd even had time to turn on the ignition.

Chapter 9

Francoeur was in considerable disarray and feeling about as foolish as his car looked when he decided, at ten o'clock Saturday morning, to call on Allan Hunger. Flight forward? Exasperation? Logical next step? He couldn't have said. Awakened by garbagemen, he'd found himself sitting shivering behind the wheel of Apocalypse on Telegraph Street. He started up the Beetle and headed for Cat Haven. Feeling feverish, he'd sat on his haunches under the shower for a good long time, then dozed off again in the kitchen in front of his bowl of cereal. Maritain, who'd dropped in to check on him, had shaken him awake.

Gregory pulled up at the address he'd found in the yellow university directory, a pink brick cottage on Josephine Street, against which stood evergreen bushes trimmed in the shape of poodle tails. *French poodles.* A high wall of unstained pine surrounded the garden, and three rhododendron bushes, redolent with fist-sized pink flowers, seemed to mark the limits of the property. A small, rotating sprinkler was meagerly watering the flourishing lawn.

When Gregory rapped on the door, using the ornamental copper knocker shaped like a woodpecker, Allan Hunger, in pajamas and silk dressing gown, appeared; he explained that the bell was out of order, but that the bird did as well as any chimes. In his right hand he held a large orange juice, and in his left, granny glasses. It saved him having to shake hands with Gregory, who looked rather seedy. Hunger checked out his visitor through small gray eyes. Gregory introduced himself and apologized for intruding at such an early hour.

"I know you! I know more about you than you think, and I'm pleased to meet you, finally," said the professor.

Then he noticed the bandage on the back of Gregory's skull.

"What happened to you? I thought you Canadians were all Catholic. You're wearing a yarmulke for Shabbat?"

Hunger laughed more heartily than seemed appropriate, as those people tend to who believe that laughing is therapeutic.

"It's the silliest damn thing," said Francoeur. "I was mugged by a paranoid musician in People's Park last night."

"You can't be too careful, Mr. Francoeur," said Allan Hunger, as he showed him into the house. "Nights can be cool in Northern California, and you never know who you'll run into."

Hunger trotted into a huge kitchen with a large skylight where giant plants and a few voluptuous black orchids bathed in generous sunlight. Coffee was perking softly on a stainless steel range, and all the accessories, from the spoons to the cushions, were various shades of red. The effect was startling. The professor offered him a mug of Mocha Java, filled it to the rim, and pushed toward him a white sugar bowl full of red granules. Francoeur was about to offer an insightful and inoffensive comment on the significance of colors when Hunger anticipated him.

"I abhor all shades of red, Mr. Francoeur, but my second wife, Joan, was so crazy about the color, she couldn't resist anything that was red, vermilion, or carmine. Now that she's left me, it would cost a fortune to replace all this ludicrous bric-a-brac. It's amazing the oddities you can inherit from a marriage. You fall for a pretty face and one day you wind up with a French provincial dining room set complete with twelve velour and gilt chairs, all immutable reminders of your third matrimonial adventure. Are you married, Mr. Francoeur?"

Gregory was caught off guard. He'd been separated such a short time, he hadn't yet adjusted to it. In any case, divorce, when it came, would not leave him with a collection of colorful gewgaws. He'd been living the life of a bachelor for only a few weeks, and he wasn't particularly happy with himself. Solitude weighed heavily on him and drove him to hasty acts. One in particular he regretted profoundly, and now he wanted to get it off his chest.

"Are you looking for a confessor?" asked Allan Hunger, as he delicately removed an egg from a pot of boiling water just as the last grain of sand ran through the timer.

"More a friend than a confessor," answered Gregory. "I'll tell you in a moment why I'm here, but first you must understand that, since I arrived in California, I've been prey to a series of unforeseen events and startling coincidences.

While the professor carefully cracked the shell of his soft-boiled egg, Gregory began to talk about his arrival in San Francisco, the furnished house he'd rented with *chammas* for curtains, the room assigned to him at the university, and the messages from Janvier. He was sipping black coffee from a crimson mug while the professor spread honey on his buttered bread and listened. He got to the part about the letter from the missionary mailed in Addis Ababa where he'd lived, the phone call from Mary Ann Wong, and his efforts to reach him and tell him about the appointment he'd made on his behalf with the Seventh Day Adventist. Gregory was not so much trying to justify his actions as to understand them. He felt like a robot advancing inexorably through a maze of signs. An inner voice kept reminding him of Ethiopia. Was it an obsession, witchcraft, or pure coincidence? He had taken on the part of the professor in this drama and he wanted out. He was afraid and he didn't mind admitting it.

"This whole mess is keeping me from my work and Terounech is your responsibility. You haven't brought her from Addis Ababa to San Francisco for my entertainment!"

"I appreciate your honesty," said Hunger, finally laying down his knife on a cherry red napkin, "and I must say I expected nothing less of you."

Francoeur was panic stricken. All of a sudden things were expected of him? Had they been manipulating him all along or had he cornered himself? In any case, he was determined to put an end to it.

"I don't understand what you mean."

Hunger smiled and said: "We needed your help." Francoeur was stunned.

"Of course, we couldn't just invite you to join us. But from what we knew of your political background, it seemed we had common interests." Hunger wiped his mouth. "We don't recruit our membership from the classifieds! That's why we're so pleased about all the coincidences and the actions you took upon yourself."

"This just won't do at all!" Francoeur was furious. "Whom do you represent? There's been a mistake. This is all a misunderstanding, you don't really know me. I have no intention of joining anything. What exactly have you dragged me into? I came here this morning to get you to pick up your Ethiopian at the airport tomorrow. Someone has to be there to meet her. It won't be me. Was it your idea to get me to drive those illegals the other night?"

"Not really. But I must admit you handled it like a seasoned pro."

"But you have no right!"

Gregory Francoeur was outraged at being so blatantly manipulated, and at his age! To be taken advantage of simply because he'd been lonely and somewhat naive. What exactly was at the bottom of all this?

"My dear Mr. Francoeur, you forget the signs. It wasn't we who put the *chammas* over your windows. You appointed yourself my assistant after you had read *my* mail. And you seem to forget you played the part so convincingly that Mary Ann Wong bought it. We didn't manipulate you at all, believe me. We simply didn't interfere. There's a war going on, Mr. Francoeur, and in times of conflict one relies on one's natural allies."

Francoeur leaped to his feet. He was staggered. Stunned. Having come to California to do a study on happiness, here he was, a few days later, involved with the political underground, awash in memories of the past, and hurtling headlong into the future all at the same time. He decided to leave. He had to be by himself, to think, maybe walk along the beach; somehow he had to regain control of his life. Hunger grabbed his arm and sat him back down.

"I'm going to tell you a story, Gregory, and only when I've finished will you be allowed to go," he said with authority.

Blushing with embarrassment and flushed with anger, the *Québécois*'s complexion quite matched the room's motif. He'd gotten himself into this and now he was too curious to leave. He had to see how it would turn out. In the yard, a dog with a deep voice barked lazily. Hunger went to quiet him. When he returned, Francoeur had regained his composure.

"You know," he said to the professor, "Addis Ababa is a city of dogs. Like Rome with its cats or Beijing with its birds. Every week the emperor used to grant audiences to foreign diplomats at his palace. At night thousands of mangy curs who'd rooted around the muddy lanes all day would come wrestle some of the banquet remnants from hyenas. The huge halls of the palace would then fill with their snarling, muted somewhat by the sumptuous gold-trimmed scarlet tapestries."

"Allan Hunger commented that Joan would have appreciated the poetry of those colors, then he headed into the living room where he put on a rock album and turned the volume up so loud it sounded like blast-off at Cape Kennedy. Signaling Francoeur to follow, he climbed to the attic, the walls of which were covered with soundproofing metal cones. The place seemed to Gregory both vast and empty. Hunger stood two chairs face-to-face at the back of the room, and from a Victorian chest of drawers, he produced earphones, mikes, and astronaut helmets, which they put on. Secluded within bubbles of mirrored plastic, covered by the deafening background music, they could communicate safely via Japanese technology. *Testing one two*. Sitting on his stool in his paisley robe with his head in the electronic helmet, Allan Hunger looked like an extraterrestrial, whereas Gregory, who was leaning forward to see better, rather resembled a giant insect.

"Can you read me?" Hunger asked.

"Loud and clear," answered Gregory.

"I'm sorry about this rigamarole, but I've been bugged so often I tend to be overly cautious. We look like fools of course, but nobody'll know. I'd also like you to keep to yourself what I'm about to say."

For thirty years Allan Hunger had been favoring the laws of the heart over those of the land. He'd been a member of every conceivable left-wing movement. It was a family tradition: his father had been accused of subversive activities along with so many others in Hollywood during the witchhunts. As a student, he'd worked on campus newspapers. *Free speech*. Then Vietnam, huge, noisy rallies, splinter groups.

"He recalled the names of battlefields, many of which have since become famous. But it was in Berkeley, he'd never forget it, that he first faced the unbridled forces of the establishment. While Allan Hunger told me his story, I was seeing a raw, unedited film of the events. I found myself in the very heart of life in America.

" 'We were neither gangsters nor bums,' the professor recalled, 'but the government forces with their jeeps, their walkie-talkies, their shields, and their weapons lost all sense of proportion. Ultimately, I think only the students had any real faith in democracy.'

"As Hunger went on I felt a growing sense of admiration. Americans of the right and the left, each believing they occupy the high ground of liberty guaranteed in their Constitution, of which they see themselves as the sole guardians, confront one another everywhere with staggering youthfulness and energy.

" 'Things turned very nasty within a few days. Each demonstration attracted more people and more cameras. The images of the conflict became more important than the principles. Those who spoke loudest became media stars and always managed to find a place under the lights. Libertarians and Communists stood shoulder to shoulder. Unlikely alliances were formed. Then, quite suddenly, the whole protest movement fell apart. The police strategy proved as effective as it was perverse: grants and big jobs to the more ambitious, handfuls of LSD to the more anxious.

" 'How could they have bought off the leaders without being lynched?' I asked.

"I was forgetting how big a country it was. Hunger explained that they'd been offered posts out East, in other famous and more peaceful universities, where they were soon forgotten. Left without leaders, the activists transformed the struggle into a drug fest, which the FBI had only to feed into.

"Had these memories brought a tear to his eye, or was that a reflection in his astronaut's helmet? His voice was sad. I kept quiet hoping he'd continue. He had turned down plum jobs and acid, he explained, and, with a group of friends, he'd decided on an alternative plan.

" 'We dropped our affiliations as if we were no longer interested in politics, but within a year we'd acquired the means to act covertly, efficiently, and without violence. We realized how absolutely absurd it was to try to fight the military industrial complex head on with placards and demonstrations. . . . That's it.'

" 'And today?'

" 'I coordinate the integration of political refugees. In Latin America I work with the churches because they're doing the best job of conciliating public opinion. It's a huge undertaking. But I have another more personal project.'

" 'Is that where Terounech fits in?'

" 'Yes, she'll be responsible for illegals from Africa. Of course, it's much harder because we have no common border and they can't row to our shores. But we'll find a way. Airports are like sieves. We might detour via Canada. Exploit the famine to touch heartstrings. You have to use your imagination.'

" 'What are you looking for?' I asked.

" 'If Washington is going to play policeman to the world, my duty is to open the country to those immigrants who are turned back at our borders. You've no doubt noticed that there are television reporters here from all parts of the world. Our enemies sponsor the news programs and think they're in control. Meanwhile, we're working on the reporters. Every time a job opens up, we try to place one of our people in the newsroom. To counter the big lie. We've made friends all over the planet. I don't believe in borders.'

" 'Terounech is to be made a television news star?'

" 'We'll try to place her in a job that allows her to travel. She'll be a reporter, not just a reader. She speaks English flawlessly. And she has all the necessary skills. The rest is a question of culture and idiom. Will you help us?'

" 'What can I do?'

" 'There'll soon be an opening in a Los Angeles station that comes in here on cable. You'll study the house style. How the reporters come across. Then you'll teach Terounech. You have four months. You'll be her tutor.'

"Here I was back in the service of the negus!

Terounech was a godsend. Wouldn't His Most Serene Highness Haile Selassie have been pleased! He who had invested so much in the education of herders and peasants. Who had encouraged them to learn foreign languages. Who had had a French governess and who had sojourned in London and traveled the world.

" 'If you could pick up our pupil at the airport tomorrow, it would really help me out. I have a meeting in Hollywood on Monday morning, and I can't be in two places at once.'

" 'I'll go. I do want to help,' I said without hesitation. 'But can I ask you one thing? A practical consideration. I had some experience organizing movements myself at one time.'

" 'You're worried about money?'

" 'And our other associates. Who are they?'

"He told me the network was made up of somewhat fewer than one hundred twenty members and that he alone knew them all. One of them, from Stanford, had perfected a form of electronic fund-raising that drew directly from the coffers of some of the major corporations. A great computer scam. He collected a miniscule share of every single market transaction. No one was the wiser. Hidden in his nylon mask, Allan Hunger was revealing himself to be an American after my own heart: the white knight, the fearless and incorruptible law man, Superman and all the other superheroes of my childhood. My empathy for these characters was such that during the period of nationalist fervor, I'd cast myself as the Defender of Justice. Among the Hollywood films that never failed to move me, there was the one in black and white about a small town newspaper editor who takes on the corrupt mayor. The screenplay must surely have been written by Allan Hunger's father. The movie opens on a tight shot of a rock crashing through the front window of the newspaper office; the name of the noble paper emblazoned across the screen. This time the gangster of a mayor has gone too far! The little guys are going to fight back and expose him for what he is. The editor calls together his reporters. Among them, Humphrey Bogart, Jimmy Stewart, . . . and Terounech.

" 'You're probably going to be watched from now on, so you have to stay absolutely clean. You'll have to be a model citizen whom the police, Internal Revenue, and Immigration can't possibly touch. They've been after me for years, and they still haven't been able to lay a hand on me. They'd have to torture me to find out anything! And they haven't resorted to that yet.' "

When he'd finished speaking, he'd removed his helmet, earphones, and mike, and he was now running his hand nervously through his damp hair. He smiled. Francoeur followed suit, removing his own fishbowl. His ears were assailed by the thundering rock music.

"I must be getting old," Hunger yelled, as he hurried down the stairs. "I have less and less patience for this kind of music."

"Do you think the cops staking you out are into heavy metal?"

Hunger answered seriously. Or maybe his humor went right over Gregory's head.

"They're thirty years old. They might well be. Do you think I should use opera instead?"

"No. On the contrary. Marshall McLuhan maintained that rock would foster global consciousness among young people. By exposing them to such tribal music, you open their minds to the universe beyond their own world."

"It may well be so," said Hunger with a playful smile.

Then he turned off the stereo. The silence was deafening. When they again became aware of normal sounds, they found themselves rather awkwardly silent. Francoeur tried to draw the professor into a discussion about modern theories of music and communication, but the joys of abstract reasoning didn't particularly seem to attract Hunger. Californians are not very inclined to confront one another over ideas. They prefer not to contradict their guests. Pacific Politeness.

Gregory took his leave from the red kitchen after having agreed to a three-way meeting in the next few days. He'd arrived with a bowed head and a guilty conscience; he was climbing back into Apocalypse with a mission! He'd have to give the professor's objectives some thought, but he knew that at last he was riding the crest of the wave for the greater good of humanity. Suzanne would have been proud of him.

"I don't really remember what I did that Saturday afternoon. A run out to the flea market, certainly. I was looking for an original present for Terounech, but nothing looked very appropriate. All possibilities seemed mere trinkets, none of them worthy of an Ethiopian princess. Maybe later I did go to the Botanical Gardens, where witnesses claim to have seen my car, but it certainly wasn't to plan my "crime" as my rap sheet suggests. Then I drove around the hills above the city to compose myself. I'd been thrown abruptly from dream to reality. Was I expected to give up my research and my grant money and become communications tutor to a young African woman I hadn't even met? Could I handle both jobs? I thought I might start my research by sorting through the surveys on motivation done at Southern California and at Illinois over the last two years. It would be useful and at the same time allow some free time for Terounech.

"Night fell. I killed an hour or so wheeling a shiny cart up and down the aisles of the Park'n Shop on Derby Street, not far from the municipal park. I wanted to prepare a feast for our delegate from the third world, but all the food on the shelves made me nauseated. In my previous incarnation, Suzanne used to do the shopping. My specialty was cleaning up. Still, I did buy a few tins for the cats. The event was worthy of some ceremony. For us: champagne, fancy cold cuts, and fruit.

"Instead of entering Cat Haven, I stopped by Maritain's. He had a card game going with a group of friends and invited me to join them. In the kitchen, while he was putting my bags into the fridge, I told him I was expecting a lady friend from far away and that she'd be staying with me. That was fine, he could relate to that. He was thinking of cohabitation himself: there was nothing I could say to clarify things, and I lost fifty dollars at blackjack before I left.

"That night Lucifer slept next to me. In the morning there were three drops of blood on the pillow. I thought nothing of it, not being of a superstitious nature. Like my American friends, I like to call a spade a spade."

Chapter 10

In the lighted passageway leading from the parking lot to the terminal at San Francisco International Airport there was an exhibition of art borrowed from private collections on the theme of Transportation through the Ages, ranging from the locomotive to the birch bark canoe. The most fascinating piece was a model of a 1950's car the size of a suckling pig enameled in a high gloss candy pink and powder blue. It looked delicious. Having chosen it as his favorite of the dozens of items exhibited in glass cages beside the movable sidewalk, Francoeur kept coming back to it. He devoured it with his eyes. Its rounded lines and yummy colors reminded him of his childhood piggy bank. Every time his mother won a tournament, he'd get a dollar. His dad would give him the same amount whenever he hit the jackpot: a Larousse encyclopedia, bookcase included, sold to a family of illiterates. Georges-Henri maintained that they could achieve by osmosis the education they'd never received. In any case there were the illustrations. Hadn't Gregory himself discovered the world leafing through dictionaries? But nobody was around to fill his piggy bank anymore. Would he ever grow up?

Gregory patiently awaited the arrival of the Pan

American flight from New York. First there'd been a thirty minute delay. That had stretched into an hour and a half, owing to a storm sweeping across the Midwest, the supervisor had explained. The plane should probably have rerouted via Mexico, but the pilot had decided to confront the eye of the storm. Francoeur had become extremely sleepy by the time the arrival was finally flashed on the screen. All he had to do now was to pick out Terounech in the crowd of passengers.

He'd thought to make himself a small sign, like those used by bellhops, and was holding it aloft. Dressed in sports clothes and old beat-up sneakers, Gregory looked like a retired minister meeting a delegation of church women. But what would *she* look like? Like an overwhelmed au pair in stasis? Like a massive case of mastitis? Like an elegant socialite, tea-room groomed and witless? *Tchai. Bikieri. Kebe.* Words he'd used daily for years and then forgotten were coming back to him. Did she belong to the Amharas, a proud-looking people, aquiline nose, soft hair, caucasian features, soft brown complexion? Or was she black and squat like the women of the Gallas? The descendant of queens or of slaves? He could remember the small, timid girls who used to sit at the back of the class at the University of Addis Ababa, wrapped in their *chammas* like ripe fruit. Only one had sometimes dared to look directly at him and smile broadly. Had she wanted him? Was she being insolent? How can one recognize contempt on a foreign face?

Almost a third of the passengers had left the plane and he was still looking for Terounech. He wondered if the Protestant preachers who'd given her refuge had tried to convert her. Insidious. Perhaps she belonged to the great Copt culture of Alexandria? Would she be wearing traditional dress?

"Crazy ideas were running through my mind. Rather than holding my sign aloft like a fool, shouldn't I be carrying a pair of testicles in each hand? That's the traditional Dankali way of proposing marriage! In fact, in times of paucity some warriors would collect their prizes from the wombs of pregnant women. Baby lottery. A cruel practice born of the desert where, in economies of scattered blades of grass and poor, sulfurous soils, any male wishing to procreate must even the tally of the quick and the dead. I would have opened my hands and presented my high plains princess with the dried organs of some hapless white hunter, disembowled under the blazing sun. Then we'd have honeymooned at the headwaters of the Nile."

The scenario could not have been more out of place. The typical Boeing traveler, alligator attaché case in hand, trench coat thrown over the shoulder, soft felt hat tilted back, keeps his precious jewels in silk. *Of course.* And Gregory, self-involved as he was, had brought to their airport neither dried testicles, nor juicy fruit, nor odiferous blooms, nor creamy chocolates. He was ashamed of himself, and the longer he waited the more embarrassed he became.

For her part, the reason the Ethiopian hadn't shown was that she simply hadn't left her seat. She felt no urge to hurry as the other passengers bullied one another getting down their hand luggage and heading out. Terounech, whose long trip had left her dozy, had so far refused even to speculate about her involvement with Allan Hunger.

During the stopover in New York, a representative of the mission had kindly met her at John F. Kennedy Airport. During their conversation she learned that a peace group had paid for her trip and that the companion job was just a white lie. At the time, Terounech had been profoundly disappointed. She had gotten used to the idea of spending her days pushing a wheelchair up and down a sunny seaside boardwalk. Hadn't she done enough for the revolution? Couldn't they just leave her alone? The missionary had been unable to say if Allan Hunger planned to involve her in political activities. Terounech longed for silence and solitude. She closed her eyes. A stewardess asked if she was all right. All the other passengers had left.

"We've landed in San Francisco; is anyone meeting you?"

Terounech smiled and nodded. Nervously she made her way down the aisle between the seats all facing in different directions. Her hair was short; she was wearing a beige suit, and gold earrings from her country dangled from her ears. Colonel Gebre Miriam, who'd been her lover for some months, had nicknamed her the "cheetah." Like boy scouts, revolutionaries also need their totems. She shook away the memories of her ex-lover, felt better, and decided to view the passage from the plane to the terminal as a birth experience. Thus Gregory saw her delivered, just as she'd been about to despair, an image both of strength and of distress: Terounech was taking her first steps into a new life.

"Mr. Allan Hunger, I take it," said the African woman.

She came up to him. Standing alone in the waiting room, his little sign in his hand, Gregory was almost paralyzed.

"I must have looked retarded. I was stunned by her arrival and could only stare, slack-jawed and stupid. Instead of offering her my hand, I bowed from the waist as low as my body would allow. Fair princess, I salute you! Then, miraculously, I remembered the inexhaustible litany of Amharic salutations.

" 'Terounech? *Ichy. Denasteling* Terounech! *Denasteling guetouch! Dana no? Dana no . . . ?*'

"She bowed back gracefully, a smile on her generous, finely chiseled lips. Then she put an end to the ritual.

" 'I'm flattered, Mr. Hunger, but that's quite enough fuss, thank you. I didn't leave Addis Ababa yesterday to find myself in a salon of the old *ghébi* today! The emperor is dead; God rest his soul. The revolution liberated all of us, peasant and princess alike, and anyway, I thought I was in San Francisco!'

"Her voice was warm. She spoke a bit quickly, but that could be corrected. Her British accent gave it a theatrical quality I'd have to think about. All these things occurred to me as I was reaching for her bag. Then I pulled myself together.

" 'I'm sorry to disappoint you, but Professor Hunger had pressing business in Los Angeles. He asked me to meet you and to make sure you got settled, since I once spent some time in your country. My name is Gregory Francoeur.'

"I held out my hand to her and she held it while she questioned me.

" 'Francoeur? That's not a very American sounding name, is it?'

" 'You're right, I'm almost as new to California as you are. I'm involved in a research project at the university. I'm a Montrealer, Quebecois born and bred.'

" 'Ah, you're Canadian?' she asked in sing-song French.

" 'You might say that.'

" 'You wouldn't be a Jesuit by any chance?' She straightened her shoulders as she asked.

" 'Not at all,' I answered, 'are you Catholic?'

" 'Muslim,' she said, as if it were obvious, 'but I've often heard of the Canadian Jesuits who used to run the University of Addis Ababa.'

" 'There weren't just Jesuits!'

" 'It used to be said that it was hard to tell the Jesuits from other Canadians. They wore laymen's clothes and drank like laymen.'

" 'That's true,' I replied, 'the negus preferred them to be dressed as laymen to avoid religious tensions. He was very astute.'

" 'You knew the emperor better than I,' said Terounech."

They made their way to the baggage area. The young woman was pleased to have met someone who knew her country. Gregory felt the responsibilities of being a family man. The delivery had been easy and the baby was already taking its first steps. Terounech commented on the luxurious appointments of the terminal.

"I spent my childhood near Saint-Georges Square in a big, white, two-story house with a tin roof that sang during the monsoon. It had a large, wooden veranda, bordered by eucalyptus."

"You'll find eucalyptus here," Gregory interjected, then he asked: "What did your father do?"

"My mother's husband was a soldier. An officer in the National Guard. He was killed in a skirmish on the Somalian border. My mother was pregnant with me at the time. He was much older than she. I don't even have a picture of him. It's almost as if he never existed."

While they'd been examining the family album,

the bags had begun to file by on the endless conveyor belt like so many ducks in a shooting gallery. Terounech pointed out a leather suitcase and Gregory grabbed it. Then came a metal reinforced trunk she'd had made in the Mercato. The thing weighed a ton and Francoeur wrenched his back lifting it.

"Not as young as I used to be," he said with a pained smile.

He rented a baggage cart and preceded her, limping slightly, out to the parking lot where the Beetle was waiting. Terounech seemed very self-possessed; Hunger had made a good choice. He found himself admiring what he'd make of her.

"I'm very glad I was asked to come and meet you," he said to her.

"You're very kind, Mr. Francoeur, but you should know that I'm extremely apprehensive and dying of exhaustion."

She stopped in front of the exit to the parking lot, forcing him to turn.

"Do you know what's expected of me?" She looked concerned.

"Nothing you can't handle, I promise you. But I think it would be appropriate for Professor Hunger to explain what he has in mind. You'll be seeing him later in the week, I'm sure. In the meantime we'll get you registered at the university.

He sensed that Terounech let herself go all of a sudden. She seemed to put herself entirely into his hands. He introduced her to Apocalypse and apologized for its dilapidated condition.

"Why that's a historical car, didn't you know?"

Terounech reminded him that even though he owned a dozen Rolls-Royces, the negus and his Pekinese dogs had been driven from his palace to prison in a secondhand Beetle.

Amused, Gregory jammed the trunk into the backseat and put the two leather bags under the hood.

"You'll see," he said, turning the ignition key, "Allan Hunger's a good man to work for."

Then he let out a "Welcome to California!" that would have brought a flush of pride to any one of the City Fathers. Gregory put the car into gear and proceeded to the gate where he paid for the parking. Terounech was quiet, her chin resting on her graceful hand, her knees drawn up under her linen skirt. She had wanted an outfit that wouldn't attract attention and had bought this suit from the Armenian dressmaker who'd once sewn for her mother. Forget the bad times. Stop thinking. Just follow. Change plans. Who was this Francoeur? Somewhat lanky, self-conscious in his every move, he looked at her surreptitiously the way the *farenghis*, the foreigners used to in the Café Ménélik when she would go there with her friends to eat ice cream.

"I kept quiet and left the Ethiopian to her thoughts. I took the ramp to route 101 north and nosed Apocalypse into the uninterrupted flow of vehicles circulating like red and white blood cells, occasionally veering off from the main artery to side arteries leading into one of San Francisco's suburbs.

"In front of us the skyline stood out against the night, vaporous and luminous, wrapped in great banks of fog that had come up from the ocean to rest against the hills. Now and then Terounech would close her eyes, not so much against the glare of headlights as from exhaustion. I saw her shiver. I told her the story of my return to Europe from Ethiopia, and of our arrival in Marseilles

aboard the *Jean Laborde*. Suzanne and I had been so ter-
rified by the noise and the agitation of the docks that we'd
literally crouched down in the taxi like a couple of frightened wild animals.

" 'And I must say, although we thought we'd left
Africa behind, Africa never leaves one, not its light, its
sounds, or its scents. You can't fight it.'

" 'I appreciate your solicitude, Mr. Francoeur,'
Terounech said slowly, 'and your Marseilles story tells me
two things: one, you're married; the other, you feel you
can put yourself in my shoes and understand me. I'll answer you in the same vein: I've been engaged, and you
could never put yourself in my place. You have your post-
cards; I have my nightmares.'

Gregory said nothing. They continued in silence
with only the sound of the tires on the pocked asphalt.
Terounech was looking straight ahead. She didn't notice
the shiny limousines that passed them. When her anger
had abated she added:

"I've just come from a country that you once knew
but that no longer exists. I've no intention tonight of going
over the story of Lenin in the Land of Sheba. But believe
me, the people paid a high price to satisfy the myths of the
twentieth century."

Images she'd wanted to forget crowded into her
mind: friends dead and mutilated, pointless carnage.

"Exactly why did you choose to come to California?" he suddenly asked.

"I don't know. For my children maybe."

Then she added impatiently: "Are we getting close
to the hotel? My biological clocks are going crazy. I
crossed eleven time zones coming here. Theoretically, I'm
younger now than when I started out!"

The lights were bright in the concrete corridor leading from the city to the long bridge across the bay. Terounech commented that more power was spent lighting San Francisco on a single night than was used in Ethiopia in an entire year.

"Indignation is pointless. No one listens."

"It's not indignation. I notice and I'm amazed. I wonder what justice there is in all this. Why was I born in Africa and you and these millions of others, in North America? Why do they have all these riches from birth like the children of emperors?"

"It's true, people here have the future served to them on silver platters like pieces of Boston cream pie. . . . Do you want anything to eat?"

"I want to sleep until I can no longer bear to be lying down!"

"We'll be there in about ten minutes. We get off at the next exit," Gregory explained. "You'll stay at my place for now. Later, we'll see."

Lucifer was sitting in the living room when Terounech first stepped into Cat Haven. The cat followed them up the stairs and into the room Gregory had prepared for his guest and where he gratefully put down the bags and the trunk. Lucifer brushed affectionately against the Ethiopian's calves and slipped under the bed. Terounech asked her host to let the animal stay with her.

"All cats have an Ethiopian ancestor," she said. "Maybe my scent reminds him of distant Abyssinia."

Francoeur bade her good night and retired to the kitchen to have a bite and to think. Everything would seem to keep us apart, he thought, race, age, culture, religion, language, and yet here we are, together in the promised land! He took out the bottle of champagne he'd left in the refrigerator and opened it with care. As he en-

120   Jacques GODBOUT

joyed his solitary sipping, Terounech was already sound
asleep, and perhaps in the depth of her sleep she could
hear the voice of an ancient matriarch telling her again,
as she had heard it in her youth, the story of the Imperial
Family. In the time of Addis.

*In those days, the earth was very small and as
flat as an ingera pancake. Balkis, the queen of
Sheba, ruled over the kingdom of Aksum and
all the southern lands of the Arab peninsula.
She was happy, young, and avid to learn
everything. When word of King Solomon's
reputation, having traveled the seas, the
forests, and the deserts, finally reached her,
she wanted to meet him. He was said to be
just, rich, powerful, and generous. And Solomon served only one God.*

*So the queen decided to leave her country
and to travel to Jerusalem leading a caravan
whose horses and camels were burdened with
sumptuous gifts: fragrant aromatics, gold and
silver jewelry, polished ivory, rare animals, including a pair of gelada monkeys who strode
back and forth in their large bamboo cages
parading their long, dark capes.*

*In those days the sovereign of Israel was
in his glory. He was thirty years old. Solomon
lived an enchanted life at the heart of an illustrious court in the midst of unsurpassed splen-
dor, surrounded by incomparable riches.
Nevertheless, when Balkis arrived, he mar-
veled at her gifts and soon fell under the spell
of his young guest's aristocratic beauty. And he*

was equally impressed by her sparkling intelligence.

The illustrious queen, herself charmed by the comeliness and graciousness of the king, asked him to instruct her in the faith of the one God and decided to remain by his side for one year. She and her entourage were settled into a palace near that of Solomon. They saw each other every morning and each day brought them closer together. Alas, a queen cannot indefinitely neglect her subjects and her throne. Sovereigns have duties of government that they cannot escape. Solomon understood this well. He considered wisely and did nothing to detain her in spite of his desire to do so. He planned a farewell feast to surpass anything ever seen before.

The banquet, which included a number of spicy dishes particularly favored by Balkis, continued so late into the night that Solomon offered the queen his chambers so that she would not have to venture forth at such an hour. The guests exchanged knowing smiles. Before she accepted, the queen of Sheba insisted that the king vow to respect her virtue. Solomon acquiesced on the condition that she in turn promise to take from the room nothing that belonged to him. This exchange of vows delighted the company.

Shortly thereafter, a very confident Balkis retired behind a screen where Solomon had had a bed prepared for her, and she promptly fell asleep. But some time later she awoke suddenly tormented by an intense thirst. A pitcher of cool water stood near at hand on a low, rosewood table. Balkis helped herself and drank deeply.

In the morning Solomon saw that his ruse had worked. He approached her gently: the vow, he said, had been broken, she had drunk of his water, he would drink from her lips. Later, when Balkis, astride her black horse, was about to leave, the king handed her a delicately tooled gold band and said: "If we are granted a son, give him this ring; it will open to him the gates of his father's palace."

Nine months later, on an island on Lake Tana where she had retired, the queen of Sheba gave birth to a young prince whom she called Ménélik. When he came of age he set out over land and sea to find his father Solomon and learn to be a king. When Balkis died, her son became King of Ethiopia, first of the dynasty of the Solomonids.

Chapter 11

"Everything in this place is as insubstantial as celluloid. One day my cell will be turned into a historical site (buy your tickets at the Ticketron outlet), and the school children of the region will be brought here for civics class to see, hands on, the lair of the *French rapist and arsonist*.

"Suzanne arrives today. She'll be coming directly from the airport to have lunch at the prison. The head guard will serve us a hot meal on trays brought up from the cafeteria. He has already inquired about our preferences: beer or regional chablis? What a country! This same man is also responsible for the public telephone, yet he's never objected to the prisoners' using stolen credit cards to place long distance calls around the world. "Hello Palermo?" "Hello Rio?" A single wing of this penal institution ran up a seventy-seven-thousand-dollar long distance bill last month. Why doesn't he put a stop to it? He says it's up to the telephone company to take appropriate action. Nothing in the prison rules forbids the use of stolen cards. It's not that he's against capitalists and corporations, he's a republican, but he is a defender of private enterprise. And the killers will be well guarded. "Hello New York?"

"I can just see Suzanne, mauve dress, string of pearls, standing in front of the library table where, for the last two weeks, I've been drawing up this document for my defense. *Write Aid*. Roenicke will have left us alone together. She'll page absently through the manuscript and look into my eyes as in the old days. Will we kiss? Will she give me a letter from Janvier whose silence worries me? Does she have news of my parents? Are they enjoying good weather on the Mediterranean coast?

"Suzanne will sit and we'll eat in silence while the guard paces back and forth in front of the rows of books bound in the prison's bindery. Then we'll talk while I hold her hands firmly in mine.

" 'Not even in your fantasies?' she'll ask incredulously. I'll tell her I don't know my alleged victim from Eve and that I never prowled around the laboratory. I'll say the real victim is me. The *ex-husband*.

" 'Don't you think you're better off in prison?' she'll say. 'You never were much good at domestic chores; this place is new, it's clean, it's even quite attractive. Here you are boarded and fed, you can write in peace; what more could you want?'

" 'Suzanne,' I'll answer, 'this is no time for jokes.'

" 'I'm not joking,' she'll say, 'I'm looking at you, poor, dear Gregory, and I see no evidence of change. The world, culture, economies evolve. You never do. You remain the same good scout searching for a cause, a sense of history, an all-seeing leader, global compassion. Professor Hunger crossed your path and you followed him as the disciples did Jesus in Jerusalem. As long as you're in prison, you're safe from your impulses. Maybe we can get you into a detention program for intellectuals.'

" 'Suzanne,' I'll answer, 'unlike most people, I have the determination to pursue my dreams. You just want me put away so you'll be rid of me for good. Who's this lawyer who came with you? Is he blond? Does he have a mustache? Are you getting it on? Who's going to pay his fee?'

"My brutal questions will stop Suzanne cold. On the verge of tears, she'll say she should never have come. I'll say I'm sorry. I'll plead with her. I'll win her over. She'll cry in my arms, console me, and find a way to touch Roenicke's heart. Then, apologizing profusely on behalf of the state, he'll let me out! And that'll be that!"

Although Gregory could always imagine himself thumbing his nose at reality and walking out of prison to the accompaniment of a marching band, could always invent fairy tales with himself as hero, blind, stupid fate continued to dog his days. A little before noon he learned from the Canadian consulate in San Francisco that his wife had been refused entry by American officials at Montreal International Airport. The lawyer she was with had not been detained. He was reminded by the voice on the telephone that American Immigration authorities had the right to refuse any Canadian entry into the United States without cause or explanation. The consul had tried to intercede, but he'd been asked by the embassy in Washington not to persist. Suzanne was on the list of undesirables and the computer had rejected her. Gregory recalled a Toronto writer who'd recently been refused a stay in the United States on the grounds that he'd denounced American militarism during a poetry reading. But Suzanne!

"Is it because she still goes by my name? Have I been blacklisted?"

The consul was sure that was the case. He proposed that, since he was in the area, the Quebec lawyer get in touch with a law firm in San Francisco and check out the situation.

"I knew your parents," said the consul, "and I wish I could help you."

Shattered, Francoeur accepted his offer to arrange a meeting with the authorities early in the week.

"Our separation seemed so natural that Suzanne and I had never bothered to ratify it in court. Now the American government was about to impose a divorce, concretely fixed in time and space. By shoving its nose into our affairs, Washington was turning a melodrama into a tragedy."

For the first time, Gregory felt this whole story slipping away from him. There was no way he could take on the entire machinery of the judicial system with only his journal for ammunition. In any case, hadn't he composed it solely for Suzanne's eyes? Now who was going to read it? Roenicke? The jury? In translation! Even the ace of communications was largely powerless in prison.

That afternoon *maître* Marleau, Quebec lawyer, met with Francoeur, who was seated between two killers behind a plate of bulletproof glass in the room set aside for family visits.

"We were facing each other on either side of the partition. Inches apart, we could communicate only by phone. I think he felt foolish. I don't know what Suzanne sees in him: his face is as bland as a winter's day. Maybe he's not her lover after all. I asked him to get some answers from Roenicke. Since I'm innocent of both charges, there must have been some other reason for my arrest. Maybe, if they went over the file again, he could come up with something.

" 'Read my journal as well. I'm prepared to answer all your questions, but I want to get out of here. And I'd like to find out what happened to Terounech. I haven't dared try to reach her since my arrest. She might not even realize I have been arrested. You've got to reach her and make sure she's all right. You'll find her at the Los Angeles YWCA. Don't breathe a word to anyone else, please. Tell her . . . '

"The prematurely thick-waisted *maître* Marleau set off in his three-piece suit to find Terounech, a photocopy of my journal under his arm. She'd been so happy those first few days in Berkeley. Without going into details, I had told her Allan Hunger wanted her to take up journalism. She couldn't quite understand the point, but she was delighted to be going back to college, and she registered the very next day for the history and communications courses I'd recommended.

"We toured the campus together, and then I went back to work, leaving her to explore the city on her own. I would never have thought that such a responsibility would give me so much joy. The professor had inspired me, and I was dying to introduce the Ethiopian to him. Meanwhile, based on the most recent research of Charles C. Harrod *et al.*, I put together a multifaceted questionnaire on happiness, discussed with young researchers the best ways to analyze the data we'd collect, and gave a second lecture that proved much more successful than the first. Even the Asian students smiled when I related true experiences and expounded my personal theories on how the media manipulate the political scene. It became quite obvious that the students were less interested in the "why" of things than in how they worked. A user's guide to politics. *Have a nice election.*

"Meanwhile, Terounech adapted quickly to her new environment, much as had the eucalyptus, originally from Australia, whose scent so moved us both. First planted for lumber, the eucalyptus had thrived and spread as successfully in Ethiopia as over the hills bordering San Francisco Bay. The lumber industry soon found that the ligneous tree was best suited for decoration and fragrance. Having no commercial value, huge eucalyptus have since grown wild for the sole pleasure of the senses.

"We were as happy as kids on vacation. We chattered like chipmunks. Terounech wanted to go to the movies every day. I accompanied her on a shopping trip to the Union Square district. Little by little she revealed her past activities and at times tried to justify them to herself.

"One night, as we were queued up for another movie, she said: 'I was in Rome with my mother and her new husband. He'd been made an ambassador by the feudal regime. I confess that I didn't ask any questions. I enjoyed the spectacle of life from ancient fountain to crowded *piazza*. I was enrolled at the French *lycée*. I had friends. Then the emperor was taken prisoner and civil servants were recalled from abroad. My family decided to remain in Italy. My stepfather was no longer very young, and he was skeptical about the change of regime. I felt, having taken courses in political science, that I should answer the call of the revolution.'

" 'You left your parents? . . . '

" 'I was very young, and I really didn't feel I was setting off to war. I was going to restore to the people the lands of the clergy, and to all the hope of a better life. When I arrived at the airport, soldiers were waiting. I was thrown in jail with the other diplomats, but when I was interrogated I pleaded my case well. I joined the revolutionary faction faithful to Colonel Mengistu. You know the rest. I can talk about this as though it were all in the past, but even as we stand here waiting to get into a movie, I'm still very frightened.' "

Every morning Gregory would call Allan Hunger's number and every morning he heard the same recorded message. To save precious time, he undertook the Ethiopian's professional training. She was extremely excited at the thought of joining the news team of a Los Angeles television network. The two of them devoured information at every hour of the day and on every channel, even though it tended to be repetitive. Francoeur described for her the state of things in America, the political dynamics, and the remarkable role Hunger was playing. Perhaps he was attempting, at the same time, to convince himself of the validity of the undertaking as well? He tried above all to communicate to her the phenomenal energy generated by the professor. The teams. The projects.

"I saw him as a major player, a character out of Dostoevsky. In the past he would have been at the side of Don Quixote, but Terounech knew nothing of either Cervantes or the Russian novel.
    " 'If sainthood exists outside of religious concepts, then Allan Hunger, to whom you owe your presence here, is a saint.' "

Five days later the body of Allan Hunger was found in a Hollywood villa. Saint and martyr. He'd been tortured, then assassinated. Word of his death spread through Berkeley like wildfire. That very night the media gave him his rightful place among the news briefs, between a flood and a spectacular pileup on the Pasadena Expressway. According to the press release, the police suspected members of an Asian gang. In the Los Angeles area particularly, more and more suburban youths had begun banding into yellow, black, or white gangs that warred against one another, pilfered businesses, and performed rituals. One night, thoroughbred dogs were found hanging from lampposts. The next day, the fingers of a hand were distributed through the mail.

According to the authorities, the gang suspected in the professor's death hung out in the bars and discos along Van Nuys Boulevard in the San Fernando Valley. But tens of thousands of local adolescents representing all races made up numerous, violent gangs, some with Nazi, others with satanic, leanings.

The friends of Allan Hunger, having been hastily called together, met in the theology faculty's amphitheater. Most of them refused to believe the official police story. They held to the theory that the CIA had used the delinquents to get rid of the professor. No one directly accused the FBI, but some claimed that the federal agency must have cooperated with the murderers. Allan Hunger had made a joke of their efforts for so long, and the FBI had never managed to trip him up. A Jesuit affirmed with clerical passion that the grounds upon which Hunger and the CIA had clashed could only have been political. Latin America?

Terounech attended the meeting without quite grasping the issues. Used as she was to the army's putting an end to such discussions, she was watching the door carefully out of the corner of her eye. No such thing occurred, but it was eventually suggested that all networks be immediately disbanded. Gregory intervened to introduce the Ethiopian as the last person to benefit from the efforts of Allan Hunger, to whom he had spoken on the eve of his departure for Los Angeles. He pleaded successfully for the preservation of the movement. They got home very late that night. Terounech had a hundred questions for Gregory. He teased her.

"You're getting carried away with your new role as journalist."

"It's not that, Francoeur," she said. "I have to know. How can the American administration arrange the assassination of a private citizen as though this country were under the worst kind of dictatorship?"

"I'm sure we came up with the right explanation," he answered. "But nobody said the administration was involved! There exist American policies regarding aliens and American interests in Latin America. Subordinate officers might well have taken the initiative of this operation in defense of those policies. They interpreted their mandate and, for the good of the nation, decided to blow the old radical away."

"And we walk around pretending there isn't a war going on!" Terounech exclaimed incredulously.

"These are exceptional acts," explained Francoeur, "but it is true that national security sometimes takes on simplistic proportions when it comes to political expediency. Police officers cold-bloodedly machine-gunned the headquarters of the Black Panthers; in 1970, the National Guard opened fire on students at Kent State. These actions were exhaustively examined and commented on in the press; therefore we must assume democracy is intact."

"But Allan Hunger is dead . . . ," the young woman whispered as she took Francoeur's hand. They completed the trip in thoughtful silence.

The only war to which Terounech was a witness

(Francoeur reflected correctly) was that of public statements and headlines, of editorials and letters to the editor. The newly created Friends of Allan Hunger held a press conference in the Presbyterian Church. The *Express* published two articles outlining the results of a detailed investigation that clearly demonstrated that Professor Hunger's trip to Hollywood had been politically motivated. An hour-to-hour account of his movements proved that he'd never been near the Elm Street villa in West Hollywood where his body was found. Somebody (the police?) leaked to the press copies of the FBI report that linked Hunger to the "traffic in illegal aliens." The *Los Angeles Times* claimed that, "according to reliable sources," these illegals were involved in the illicit drug trade in California. That kind of slander always has a lingering effect. Hunger faded from the front pages but, like Chinese firecrackers, harassment continued from various quarters. The professor's friends were all subjected to anonymous phone calls, impromptu visits from the Internal Revenue, and investigations at their places of employment.

The first time Terounech was stopped on the street near the university by a cop in a patrol car and taken to a police station, they simply checked her visa and her bank balance, but she was still shaking when she got back to the house. She waited for Gregory, sitting bolt upright in the living room, holding tightly to Lucifer, who'd presaged the tragedy but understood nothing of this frantic affection. ("Three drops of blood. I'm not superstitious!" Gregory had thought. Henceforth he'd be more careful.)

When he got home and saw what a state Terounech was in, he gave her rice wine and comforted her as best he could. Allan Hunger's death in no way affected her status as a landed immigrant, nor could they invoke any reason to deport her. This was confirmed by an immigration lawyer whose name they'd found in the yellow pages. Yet every evening at about seven o'clock, an unmarked car would park conspicuously nearby. Maritain noticed it first and phoned Gregory to warn him. From behind the living room curtains, he tried surreptitiously to identify the car's two occupants. It was futile. Like their car, they were indistinguishable. They usually left at about eight o'clock after speaking briefly into their radio mike. Terounech and Gregory became as nervous as cats.

"A few days after the autopsy, a funeral service was held in the chapel of Stanford University, where Hunger had studied. I was invited, along with two other people, to deliver a eulogy before the cremation. I spoke about the role the professor had played in my life during the short time I'd been in California. I invited his associates to vindicate his death by carrying on the struggle. Terounech was at my side. I declared that she and I would be eternally grateful to the true democrats of the country who were not necessarily those elected by the majority! Amen. A picture taken during my speech was printed in the local papers, including the front page of the *Daily Californian*. The gangs went wild. Or maybe it was just some young, impressionable hooligans."

White kids on shiny, whining motorcycles paraded by at sunset heaving empty bottles at the house and into the yard. Some spray-painted obscene graffiti on the brown shingles of Cat Haven before roaring off. The next morning, as they were leaving, Terounech and Gregory stumbled over the body of Lucifer, his throat slit. Terounech screamed and ran crying into the street. Old ghosts come back to haunt.

Francoeur caught up to her and swore he'd take action. But the FBI was there before he had a chance to. While he and Maritain were burying Lucifer at the back of the garden, a black car pulled up in front of the house and in a moment its four husky occupants were on the porch. The caretaker was gone in a flash. The officers identified themselves routinely and quietly suggested they talk. They began questioning Gregory in the kitchen and Terounech in the living room. Periodically they switched places. The interrogation, tense but quite civilized, lasted several hours. When it was over, not wanting to leave Terounech, Francoeur called the university to say he wouldn't be coming in. He asked the police but never found out if his phone was tapped.

"When the gentlemen had finally left, Terounech threw herself into my arms. We were like two orphans in the midst of a B-grade tragedy. This charade was pushing local color too far! I stroked her hair and gently asked her to tell me what had happened.

" 'I have to know what they asked you.'

" 'Don't make me go over all of it again,' she sobbed.

" 'Terounech, how else can we defend ourselves?'

"She was silent for a while, then she began to pace, and then, with great effort, she composed herself and sat down on the sofa as if she were about to be served tea.

" 'They were particularly interested in how I'd been contacted, why I came to the States, and my connection to some Protestant ministers who were known to them. One of them, the older one, wanted to hear about the conspirators who deposed the emperor; he was concerned about my role in the *Derque*. They read from a list the names of revolutionaries who'd studied in the States and in Canada during the sixties. They asked if I knew any of them and if they'd maintained contact with their American universities. I don't *know*! A hundred things! My sex life. Your political views. My stepfather's business in Rome. The money used by Miss Wong. My plans for the future.'

" 'You answered all their questions?'

" 'They know more about me than you can imagine! The smaller one, the one with the bad complexion, speaks Amharic! He's lived in Erythria.'

" 'That doesn't tell me what you said to them,' I persisted.

" 'I told them the simple truth. I said the revolution had made me sick. I told them I lost a sister and a cousin to the massacres and that I never wanted to have to remember the sight of all the bodies of village children again. I told them I had come here to find peace and to start over.'

"She was quiet for a moment, then she got to her feet and came to me smiling, almost pleading.

" 'Couldn't we forget about all this? Leave the city? Take a holiday?'

" 'I wouldn't want to give the impression that I was running off,' I said, hesitating, 'but I guess we could get away for a few days. In fact, it's a great idea!'

"I was suddenly quite enthusiastic."

Francoeur realized that neither of them was capable of doing any work, and that their behavior was increasingly erratic. They might as well go. He could talk to the department and reschedule a class; assign work to his research assistants. What good would it do to stay and go over the same ground, dealing day after day with Hunger's death, unable to concentrate or even to watch television, the police dramas too closely resembling their own. On the screen, Hunger's assassins, Lucifer's tormentors, were constantly crisscrossing electronic America, racing over hill and dale in helicopters and cars. Why shouldn't they do a little traveling of their own?

"The problem," said Gregory, "is that although I know nothing of the professor's network the cops won't accept that. They're bothered by my political past. I'm afraid they think I'm dangerous! They're sure to come back. I think they're more interested in me, now, than they are in you."

"That settles it, then," Terounech said with determination, "we have to leave right away."

They divided up the tasks. While she collected the things they'd need from around the house, he went downtown to the REI to rent a tent and sleeping bags. Maybe they'd permanently opt for life under the stars? He stored everything under the hood of Apocalypse and filled the tank.

"We wanted to change planets. We decided to follow the coast southward. To our left the mountains rose like so many cats arching their backs, while on the other side the spray showered lazy seals dozing on huge rocks. We traveled slowly, stopping often on ever steeper and higher slopes covered with wild orchids. Terounech delighted in the discovery of such luxuriant nature. Accustomed as she was to a desert landscape, her senses were overwhelmed. She was so relieved to find herself free between the sky and the sea, far from political harangues, that, late in the afternoon on the road to Big Sur, she insisted on going down to the beach. We left the car by the side of the road and started down a steep trail to the ocean a thousand feet below."

Facing the thunderous ocean, just when the slanting sunlight was bursting into rainbows in the spray, Terounech turned to Gregory.

"Francoeur," she said softly, "I think I'm in love with you."

The tall, old-young man looked at his hands, where age spots were beginning to show, thought with alarm that he'd have to climb back up the trail without panting, and finally smiled affectionately.

"You mustn't mistake the natural solidarity of victims for love," he said sententiously. "Here, on this wet sand, my back to the cliff and the ocean in my eyes, I'd like to believe we're the first human beings on earth. But I know it isn't so."

Terounech persisted.

"I love you because you're my past and my future, that's all."

"For me you are the present," he said with a smile.

"This is no time to teach me conjugations, Francoeur."

Terounech had long arms which she waved when she spoke. Gregory kept his by his side against the chill of the ocean breeze. When they came to each other they spun; like a weather vane in a gale, they whirled into one.

Chapter 12

While the lawyer tried to find Terounech in Los Angeles, while the consul consulted in a Russian Hill cocktail lounge, while the space shuttle Challenger landed in the California desert, and while, at the Jet Propulsion Laboratory, a laser was being perfected that could kiss a star, Gregory Francoeur was spending his third Sunday in prison in "precautionary custody." He was becoming increasingly convinced that he was a hostage in negotiations the stakes of which he couldn't comprehend. He killed the entire morning reading the two hundred pages of the *New York Times* graciously supplied by the prison administration, but it didn't cheer him up significantly. When he again refused to go and watch the ball game in the yard, the furious guard gave him only two hot dogs and a glass of milk for lunch. This persecution restored his good humor. After all, they hadn't broken him, and the fact that Roenicke was keeping him in solitary confinement could be seen as a sign of weakness on their part. Would they have arrested him if he and Terounech had not left so suddenly?

Both in their own sleeping bags, not daring to admit to rising desire, they had fallen asleep in their tent in

Pfeiffer Park, surrounded by trees older than Christianity. In the morning while hawks, silent as paper airplanes, glided in the azure sky, they became talkative, recalling ancient loves and their uneasy childhoods; exchanging, pell-mell, necessary memories. With extreme modesty they were drawing closer together.

In a roadside café built of ersatz logs, where the waiters were dressed as loggers, Francoeur confided: "My first political experience will seem ridiculous to you. It happened when I was nine years old at the corner of Chambord and Laurier in the Mont Royal district where we were living at the time. Back then, even in the French area of the city, we'd sometimes run into our enemy, the English."

"Why 'enemy'?" Terounech asked. "The English liberated Ethiopia from the Italian Fascists in 1944!"

"They were our enemy because they spoke the language of the masters. It goes back to the old story of the conquest. That day around noon a gang of them caught me and dragged me into an alley to give me a hard time. I was scared and I started screaming that they had made a mistake. I spoke their language without an accent. So they let me go."

"I don't see how that led you into politics," Terounech said with a smile."

"I never forgave them for making me lie to save my skin. It was as though I had denied my own. Think of my father, model employee of a French publishing house! I would never have wanted him to know about my betrayal.

"I was thirteen," said Terounech. "It was near the end of the term. I was enrolled, along with the other young girls from the palace, at the high school run by the Seventh Day Adventists. For weeks there'd been incredible rumors about the army. But we felt safe. Until one day during English class three officers burst in and pushed the teacher aside. They walked up and down the aisles holding an aluminum platter on which was a piece of meat so rotten the stench was nauseating. I'm sorry to bring this up while we're eating."

"It doesn't matter." Francoeur stuck his fork into a sausage surrounded by roast potatoes, fried bacon, scrambled eggs, and pieces of orange. "I'll eat later."

"While one of them forced each of us to touch the putrefying meat, the other two were telling us it was the share reserved for the collaborators of Ethiopian feudalism! And they added that such rot was still better than what the people had to eat. They invited us to come down into the street to support the revolution. The parents of some of my classmates had already been taken prisoner and these girls were crying helplessly. I was even then quite tall for my age and I blended easily into the chanting crowd headed for the university."

"Was that before you went to Rome?" Francoeur asked.

"Yes. Mother hadn't remarried yet."

"So your stepfather was sent to Rome by the revolution?"

"No, he wasn't. You're getting everything mixed up. The emperor stayed until the very end. His ministers and his cohorts disappeared on a regular basis, but he kept appointing other ministers, civil servants, ambassadors. He used to say that if the revolution was good for the people, then he was in favor of it. Little by little he was isolated, without his ever being touched personally. The people would never have stood for it. I went to Addis when he was taken captive."

"Our revolution was rather quiet by comparison," said Francoeur. "Which is probably just as well."

When they set off again, fog still hung over the countryside. Now and again the sun would briefly break through. They could sense rather than see the hills piled up like watermelons on a market stand or the brown animals grazing on gray grass along the canyons.

"Feeling better?" inquired Francoeur.

"Are you sure we're not being followed?" Terounech asked.

Gregory reassured her. As they journeyed along in the Apocalypse, the time had come to take stock.

"I want to talk about Allan Hunger," said the young woman. "He died because he always put the good of society before his personal interests. Is that right? If children were being hurt he would launch a campaign against violence?"

"And it was he who found a new way to put apartheid back into the headlines," added Francoeur.

"What did he want from me?"

"What's the use? He's dead now and so are his plans."

"I have a right to know!"

"Of course you do . . . how can I explain? He wanted you to operate an immigration network from Africa to America."

"Why? To subvert the government?" asked Terounech.

"He used to say that America belonged to the entire world. You'd have been one of a large number of people involved in a great mixing of the races. That's it in a nutshell."

Gregory had nothing more to add.

"Allan Hunger really saw himself as the conscience of the world, didn't he!" Terounech exclaimed. "And that's a sure way to make the news, isn't it?"

"You're being unfair," said Gregory.

"I am not being unfair. I'd just like to know where he got the right to make decisions affecting our happiness!"

"When you went home to Ethiopia from Rome wasn't it to transform society for the greater happiness of each individual?"

"When you were elected on a question of language," asked Terounech, "wasn't it also for the greater happiness of society?"

"So?"

"We both have to concede defeat. Hunger's would have been even more resounding. You aren't particularly happiness incarnate and neither am I. And it gets worse: we're both in exile after having helped one particular class of citizens seize power over others. We played a part in a superficial transformation. In my country a cruel but weak government was replaced by one that is cruel and strong. Some progress!"

"You're being unfair!" said Francoeur. "We had no choice but to take political action."

"That's not true, Francoeur," she smiled sadly, "and you know it better than I. The power of advertising is stronger than military power. You said so yourself. Politics are only a small part of life. We aren't here (she opened her slender hands to indicate the brilliant cinema-scope vistas unrolling beyond the windshield) for political reasons!"

"Absolutely! We're running from the authorities in the Apocalypse at forty-five miles an hour!"

"Downhill!"

They laughed. But they were wondering what

they were really doing on this winding road. The Federation of Communicators. A research project on happiness. A job as an accountant for some missionaries in Diredawa. A plane ticket, random as a lottery ticket.

"Maybe so," said Francoeur, who was loath to drop a subject before he'd exhausted its possibilities, "but a lottery ticket provided by a political organization!"

"Did we have a choice?"

"I suppose each of us was looking for a way out of an impasse."

"There are no impasses," replied the Ethiopian, "only fate."

The Apocalypse swerved. Francoeur deliberately skimmed the edge of the cliff on the ocean side. This was followed by an interminable discussion on Islamic fatalism. On the place held by John Wayne in the collective unconscious and on that held by Tom Cruise in the imaginations of young girls. They moved on to the conspicuous consumerism of the white telephone, but their hearts weren't in it. The passenger suggested and the driver concurred: the institutional and societal problems that were the passion of their respective solitudes seemed to fade like trees on distant cliffs, now that they felt close to each other.

"I've always had difficulty separating my intellectual flights from my emotions. These discussions with Terounech were making me feel young again. We were stripping away the old man with his predictable reactions. I could feel the prerogatives of the heart gain the upper hand.

"When we were still a few hours from the next town, the fog had become so dense we couldn't even see the suspended bridges we were crossing. Meanders, promontories, and rock faces as concrete as fate rose up before us. We tried to cut inland to the highway. In vain. Here, too, cars crept along with their headlights on. In the distance the outskirts of Los Angeles looked ghostly, as if conceived by Disney Studio artists. As we drew closer the interchanges faded into a curious yellowish soup composed of ocean mist and pollution. Here and there in the fields, neon billboards glowed like luminous jewels strewn by the roadside. The fabulous landscape commanded silence and kept us glued to the windshield absorbing it all."

The police claimed to have found Allan Hunger's body at 740 Elm Street in West Hollywood. Francoeur couldn't conceive of stopping in Los Angeles without paying his respects on that quiet suburban street lined with low, pink stucco houses, each fronted by a flowering palm. *Greetings from California.* First he passed the bungalow at funeral speed. He wanted to check out the site that had been the professor's tomb. As if it might bring him back to life! It's always hard to believe in the death of someone close when the body is disposed of without being exposed. At the service before the cremation a recent photograph had simply been placed on the coffin. "Why not carve his social security number on the urn!" Gregory had thought. He parked the car by the curb. The sidewalk was already strewn with the petals of Japanese cherry trees. Terounech remained seated in the Apocalypse.

In the gloomy night, frigid air blowing in from the ocean chilled him to the bone. The street was crushingly dull. The incriminated house was distinguishable from its neighbors only by the Century 21 sign and the two dozen newspapers in plastic wrappers that littered the lawn and porch. The garage housed a black car without plates. The yard was empty but for the rusted remains of a long-abandoned swing. By climbing onto the low brick wall surrounding the patio, he could see a pilot light flickering in the depths of the kitchen. It was easy to surmise that the professor had been killed elsewhere and his body brought here to throw off the local authorities. Perhaps the house even belonged to the FBI. *Why not?* Federal agencies own secret ranches, undercover offices, unmarked cars. Why not a house in West Hollywood for the disposal of overactive activists. We've all seen that sort of thing in the movies. Besides, he could find no trace of graffiti on the walls. And gangs almost always sign their work. What an amateur job, thought Gregory!

"When I got back to the car, Terounech was standing on the wet and worn roadway, waiting for me. She'd put up the collar of her white jacket and shoved her hands deep into the pockets. She was studying my face.

" 'What's eating you, Francoeur?'

" 'Allan Hunger has just dematerialized, and he's taken a part of my life with him. I don't know what I was hoping to find here. A sign, maybe. I'm still not even sure what he took from me when he left.'

" 'The best years of your life, maybe,' joked the Ethiopian.

" 'I barely even knew him!'

" 'Your dreams of adventure, your desire to change the world, and this depressing street is all he left you. And you're disappointed, admit it.'

"A car passed, splashing mud and light. Then the street sank back into its lugubrious silence.

" 'It's true. I wanted to make dull reality correspond to my imaginings.'

" 'You're talking like a book, Francoeur.'

" 'Is there anything wrong with that?' I asked testily.

" 'You're in the movie capital of the world and you're talking like a book!'

"She took me by the arm and led me around the Beetle, which, it seemed to me, had, like my spirits, somewhat sagged under the weight of the trip, and pushed me inside. Then she slid behind the gray and red steering wheel and told me to shut my eyes. She would drive to a hotel; there must be one somewhere nearby. When I'd closed my eyes and she'd put Apocalypse into gear, she asked softly:

" 'Is it your own death you're so worried about?'

"It wasn't so much a cruel question as a logical conclusion. Irrefutable. Implacable. What was to become of my life? A quiet career as a California zombie? *Spaced out?*

" 'While you find us a place to stay, I'm going to pass away, and I'll resurrect only when you've found a motel. Or in three days, whichever comes first.'

"At my age, I thought, it's not that the effort's so hard, but the recuperation takes forever."

With that thought in mind, Gregory fell asleep leaning against the vibrating door. Suzanne was the only person on earth with whom he could share the true weight of his emotional turmoil, but Suzanne had abandoned him. While he dreamed, Terounech drove the boulevards. He never knew how long the search lasted. When he awoke, Terounech was lightly kissing his forehead. "Only children and old men get kissed on the forehead," he thought. Then he unloaded their bags and signed them in as Mr. and Mrs. G. Francoeur under the watchful eye of a skeptical desk clerk. Of course the Apocalypse didn't look any too respectable.

The room was on the third floor of a black metal and cement building, ersatz Spanish mission, with a bar and a chapel under the campanile, cactus and a horse trough in the courtyard. From the cast-iron balcony they saw that the fog had finally lifted, and they could hear the prostitutes on Sunset Boulevard soliciting passing motorists in the increasingly noisy and hot night. Gregory could just feel himself sinking into the mattress when Terounech suggested a walk around the neighborhood. She wanted to feel the pulse of Hollywood, breathe in the dust of the stars.

At midnight, in front of the Chinese Theater, the Ethiopian was shining a flashlight from one famous actor's footprint to another. The patio was crowded where for fifty years film heroes and heroines have left their hand- and footprints in the cement. It's normal when you live in the ephemeral to want to leave concrete traces. As he wandered from one to the other, Francoeur discovered he wore the same shoe size as Humphrey Bogart, which surprised him because he knew the actor had been much shorter than he.

"Big heart, small feet," as they say back home.

Terounech had coined the saying on the spot, to cheer him up. She was being matronizing.

"How about you, have you found prints your size?" he asked.

"Marilyn Monroe, Jean Harlow, Doris Day, Jane Russell . . . foot-wise I'm all of them. But who were they?"

"How do you explain to an African born on the other side of the planet, on the high Abyssinian plateau, in Saint George's Square, about the fleeting black-and-white images of baroque celluloid godesses? How to explain that we were standing under the great American big top? That elephants didn't forage here but were trained to curtsey for the amusement of children? That snakes threatened no one, assuming instead the shape of handbags? That gazelles grazed on the wild grass of hills dominated by the mansions of film stars? That the natives of this village awaited merely the glance of a producer in the hope that they might slip before the camera into an American story? Terounech was born of a letter forgotten on Allan Hunger's desk and here we were arm in arm amid the curious in this mockery of a shrine! Holidaying pilgrims carried lighted candles and, dripping a few drops of hot wax on the cement, stood them there reverently. Vigil lights of silver screen veneration! Douglas Fairbanks Jr. alone was honored with a dozen flames left by a family of respectful Mexicans. *Viva Zapata!* Siren blaring, a patrol car roared by, followed by a white stretch limo headed for the exclusive clubs of Beverly Hills. Terounech came close and pressed up against me. She was looking at me with eyes that seemed so dark and new that I found myself crying silently, as men do.

" 'You're as salty as the sea,' she said, as she kissed my cheek.

" 'I always cry at the movies,' I said.

"Pop porn."

Chapter 13

Over a period of forty-eight hours, the room in the motel *La Reina de los Angeles de Porcuincula* saw Terounech and Gregory expend the energy of a lifetime. Then, in the morning light, after furious discussion, slow caresses, and tearful smiles, they both accepted the inevitability of separation. For a long time they remained face-to-face in the cactus yard, feeling at once full and empty, hand in hand, trying to condense into each sentence hundreds of thoughts and feelings. Terounech refused to go back up north. She wanted to live freely, no longer to be bullied by FBI agents or missionaries, or dragged into morbid adventures. She was in America, she said. She could just as easily learn a profession in Los Angeles as in Berkeley. She dreamed of melting into the crowd, as anonymous as a child. If necessary she was willing to serve breakfast in one of the coffee shops that seemed always in need of a waitress. To set his mind at ease, she promised to continue studying, and she even offered to be the network's eyes and ears in Los Angeles. She owed him at least that much loyalty.

"We concurred that if our memories were out of

synch, our futures were even more disparate. What had she to gain in coming back with me? Only because we'd both been orphans alongside the Pacific had I become her godfather, her mentor, and her lover. But I could just as easily have been her father! Any rationalization will do when comfort is needed.

" 'And we'll call!'

"Always the technological solution, I thought, the electronic substitution. You're proving to be precisely the petit bourgeois Suzanne always accused you of being. Not a single grain of madness left in you! Politics have ruined your affectivity, and now you're incapable of the least flight of fantasy. You no longer know how to live, to dare, to laugh. You're going to return docilely to Frisco-work-sleep. There's a job waiting for you, a serious study of happiness, isn't that more enriching than a small, personal joy? Students will be sitting in class next Thursday; you have a sense of duty and of history; you mustn't disappoint them. A place for everything; everything in its proper place. *Have a nice life*.

"I caught a last glimpse of Terounech through the rear window of the Beetle. She was standing tall and proud in a fire red sweater, waving her arms, in front of the YWCA on Flower Street in Los Angeles. Then a car came up behind me, between her image and the memory of her. The light turned green. *Go, man!*"

Gregory went right back to Cat Haven as quickly as possible via the Central Valley Freeway that rips as straight as a canal through irrigated farmlands. On either side of the Apocalypse in the luminous mists of March, mechanical sprinklers nourished the uniform furrows. Here and there one-eyed tractors like giant cyclops crossed the delicate curtains of spray. The fertilized earth was beginning to yield its bounty of spinach and straw-berries.

Much later, when he reached the pass at Altamont east of San Francisco with its hills covered in tall, white wind generators, he saw that the spinning blades were only blades and realized that his veins no longer held a single drop of quixotic blood!

"The authorities understand the subsequent events much better than I. When I finally got back to Piedmont Street, Maritain was waiting on the doorstep as though he'd been expecting me. He helped me with my bags, took two beers from the fridge, and, as we sat in the kitchen, he began gently to interrogate me: where had I been?

" 'The Friends of Allan Hunger have had a couple of meetings,' he said. 'They missed you. You said you'd take on certain responsibilities.'

" 'I know,' I answered, as I took a pull from the cold bottle, 'but there's one thing I learned from the professor: you should never act quickly after a tough set-back. It's better to fade out of sight and let people forget about you. Disappear into the woodwork.'

" 'You didn't tell anyone,' said Maritain, looking hurt. 'We thought you were pulling a fast one.'

"I started pacing the tiled floor and counting the geometric figures as I stepped on them. Then I leaned on the warm porcelain surface of the gas stove and emptied my beer bottle in three gulps. I was trying to figure out what Maritain was driving at.

" 'What exactly did they think I was up to?'

Maritain put down his beer and scratched the back of his head in apparent embarrassment. " 'You know, Gregory, over the last several years Allan Hunger managed to survive a number of betrayals. He had an in-

stinct for shaking tails and foiling plots. He always set up
a screen between his activities and the cops.'

" 'Yes,' I said, 'he told me all about it.'

" 'So, when you disappeared like that, we found it
strange.'

" 'Why?'

"But I really didn't want to hear Maritain go on.
His look was hardening slowly, and he was turning pale.

" 'The professor's troubles started shortly after you
arrived. Some say you were answering the phone in his
office.'

" 'Of course. It was my phone too!'

"I was becoming upset.

" 'Others found it curious that you were the last
person to speak to him before his disappearance. By your
own admission he even told you he'd be in Hollywood the
following Monday.'

" 'So?'

"Maritain seemed delighted to report, like so
much gossip, the suspicions of the Friends of Allan
Hunger.

" 'So,' he said, 'we felt perhaps you weren't entirely innocent. Maybe your job was to put an end to a fine
adventure. Allan Hunger had a weakness for exotic
revolutionaries, and that's how he saw you; he fell into the
trap like a child.'

"I stood shaking my head in denial as he went on.

" 'Didn't you try right from the start to imper-
sonate him? We, Hunger in particular, should have been
more careful! His death allowed you to bring the members of the network together and expose them. And after
we'd all been drawn into the light, you suddenly disappear.'

" 'You don't really believe what you're saying?!'

"I was paralyzed with anger. Maritain got up, he was looking at me suspiciously. I grabbed the empty beer bottle he'd left on the table and heaved it down the small hallway; it broke with a hollow sound against the living room wall. The caretaker went out the back door without turning around, leaving me alone with his accusations."

Francoeur never really ate or slept after Maritain's visit. He hardly dared look outside. He felt dirtied and cheated. The next day, when he was getting ready to take a bath, the cop who'd driven him to the hospital after the mugging in People's Park rang his doorbell. When he let him in, he noticed Maritain on the sidewalk across the street watching his house.

The authorities were worried about Terounech's disappearance, the officer told him, and he asked Gregory to come to the station with him.

Francoeur asked if he could quickly finish bathing and dressing. Being taken in like this might just be his chance to prove his good faith! Would they arrest an informer! That's why he refused to reveal the whereabouts of the Ethiopian and they locked him up.

"I was transferred from a grimy office to an even sadder one; from an ancient building to a brand-new concrete one; from a gray cell to this room in a comfortable prison. I was told I could make a few phone calls. First I tried to reach Mary Wong. She must have been on some other planet. When I appealed to the department at the university, they chose, in the person of the female administrator, not to get involved. The best the Association of Communicators could do was suggest the name of a lawyer. But I still didn't know what the charge was going to be. It was at that very moment that I decided to prepare my defense by writing up an account of my adventures in California. Every day before I start to write, I greet the old Death Valley date palm that the gardeners are constantly watering because it refuses to take root in prison. Three weeks ago I left the Apocalypse in the shade of some eucalyptus in the parking lot of the police station. It must still be there."

Like Haile Selassie, he'd gone to jail in a Beetle! Wondering how the old Lion of Judea could have adapted to life behind bars, Gregory fell asleep once again in the neon light of the federal prison. In his frenzied dreams he found himself in his father's library, where he spent endless hours classifying the encyclopedias without ever getting them quite right. By eight in the morning, Marleau was waiting for him behind the glass in the visiting room. As soon as he'd been brought in, Francoeur grabbed the receiver, and before he'd even sat down, he asked what news the lawyer had brought.

"Good news and bad news," said Marleau, who nonetheless seemed quite pleased with himself in his new beige linen suit. "I spoke to Suzanne this morning, and she thinks you should accept what I have negotiated."

"How is she? Can she really not come?" asked Francoeur.

"It may not be necessary. The prosecutor has proposed a deal whereby he would be prepared to drop the rape and arson charges."

Gregory felt his heart race as if he'd just run an all-out sprint.

"Did they tell you why I'm being held? The real reasons?"

"I think it's best not to insist," Marleau answered cautiously. "Not to demand press releases or public apologies. You're being held under a number of charges that give them a variety of options. Let's just say that when they were investigating the rape, they found a newspaper clipping with your picture in the victim Cheryll Wilson's room. You mention the article in your journal. It seems the young lady had gotten herself pregnant and decided to lay the burden of her wayward ways on you. She confessed a week ago when they gave her a lie detector test."

"That's great, Marleau!" Gregory yelled into the phone. "Vindicated by a polygraph! Absolved by a needle! Pardoned on the strength of a read-out! Terrific! I take back everything I've ever written against technology! The Catholic church should put polygraph machines in all their confessionals. Think how efficient they'd become at prescribing penance!

"I see you're feeling more like your old self again." Marleau tried to humor him.

"If they've known for a week, how come I wasn't told?"

"Because they never believed in the rape in the first place," answered the lawyer. "It was just an excuse to hold you and put a scare into you. But there's more: Roenicke is prepared to trade off the arson charge against a confession of complicity in the traffic of undesirable aliens."

"That's ridiculous. I'm not going to betray the network."

"You don't have to. You know California is waging a veritable war at the Mexican border? Yesterday alone, Roenicke told me, they turned back more than two thousand illegal immigrants! On February 10th, when you transported, in a Toyota, two Salvadoran citizens sought by the Immigration and Naturalization Service for illegal political activities, you contravened articles 212C and 280A of the Immigration Act. Do you deny that?"

"Come on, Marleau," said Gregory, laughing at the other's formality, "I wrote it all up in my journal; you and Roenicke both have copies! How could I deny it?"

"Easily," answered the lawyer. "You can't testify against yourself, and the only incriminating piece of evidence is, in fact, your journal."

"All right, so I deny it."

"And Roenicke presses the charge of arson already pending," Marleau explained patiently.

"What do you suggest?"

"I went to Los Angeles on Sunday, and I met Terounech Téklé where you said she'd be. She's a helluva good woman! She's prepared to turn herself in and face deportation if it can help you out of your fix."

Gregory remained silent for a moment. He was trying to relive the trip that had separated them. Landscapes and feelings. Could he admit that, in his way, he too was in love?

"But Terounech's papers are in order," he said. "What would be the point of bringing her back out into the open? I'm the one the INS is after, aren't I?"

"I think Ms. Téklé made that statement hoping you'd get the message that she wants to help you."

"What would I be facing if I confessed to transporting the illegals?"

"You're an alien yourself, here on a temporary work permit. They'll revoke it. And for helping out the immigrant running clergymen, you'll be deported."

"All right then, let them deport me and happiness be damned! I don't need a research project to be happy."

"You admit your actions and accept their consequences?"

Gregory wanted to know if he'd ever be able to enter the States again. Visit New York or a beach in Florida.

"You can have your file reviewed every five years, but there's no guarantee they'll wipe it clean. As you know, the Immigration Department is very rigid."

Gregory thanked Marleau, mimicked a handshake from behind the glass, and hung up the phone. The lawyer fairly pranced off. Francoeur was escorted back to his quarters, where he grabbed a yellow legal pad and began to write feverishly under the indifferent eye of the guard.

"So Terounech did not lose herself in the back alleys of Venice! She didn't meet a crazy coke freak of a director. Maybe this very minute she's washing blue dishes in a Chinese restaurant? She's probably decided to carve out a piece of Utopia for herself in California, but what can she really hope for from this country?

"I'll have to explain to her that neither she nor I will ever really be part of the richest nation in the world. What if she is looking for a promised land? I'll show her winter, gray skies, discomfort, instability, the forests; I'll ask her to marry me, and Suzanne and Marleau will stand up for us; Janvier will sculpt a cake, and, on our honeymoon, we'll visit my parents in Provence! And if I can still manage an erection when she applauds, we'll have a child and we'll call him Bellatchow ('Beat them up'), in memory of People's Park, U.S.A.

"Bellatchow Francoeur will be the first heir to the Planetarian Dynasty; he'll know how to combat effectively against the armageddons taking shape right now in California laboratories.

"Let them burn!"

Jacques
GODBOUT

Jacques Godbout is a contemporary *Québécois* writer who has published poetry, novels, and essays and is also a filmmaker. Born in Montréal in 1933, and educated at the Université de Montréal, he published his first collection of poems in 1956 and two years later began to work for the National Film Board of Canada. Since then he has divided his time between writing and filmmaking. He founded the journal *Liberté* in 1959 and has taught at the University of California, Berkeley, the Université de Montréal, and in Ethiopia. His prize-winning novels include: *L'Aquarium* (Prix France-Canada, 1962), *Le Couteau sur la Table* (L'Academie française, 1965) and *Salut Galarneau* (Prix du Gouveneur-General, 1968). His most recent novels are *L'Isle au Dragon* (1976), *Les Têtes a Papineau* (1981), and *Une Histoire Américaine* (1986).

Yves Saint-Pierre teaches English at Dawson College, Montréal. He received his MA in Comparative Canadian Literature from the Université de Sherbrooke, Sherbrooke, Québec. Saint-Pierre has translated the telaplay *La Piastre*, by Pierre Dagenais, and the play *La Visite des Sauvages*, by Anne Legault. His poetry has been published in several Canadian quarterlies including *The Alchemist*, *Grain*, *Waves*, *Zimergy*, *The Amphora*, and *Up Front*, an anthology of Toronto poets.